Mail Order Sarah

Book Two of
Sweet Willow Mail Order Brides

Charlotte Dearing

This is a clean, wholesome love story set in late 19th century Texas. The hero is strong and independent, a happy bachelor living alone until a young boy asks for his help. That day he becomes the caretaker of six orphaned boys aged twelve and younger, and his life is never the same.

Chapter One

Noah Bailey

Noah woke with a start, unsure if he'd imagined the plaintive cry of a child. He lay in bed, staring into the darkness. Some of the boys had bad dreams sometimes. And no wonder. They'd had a tough start in life. He listened intently, ready to get up and go calm the boy if need be.

A moment before he'd been in the middle of a mighty fine dream, sweet-talking a pretty lady, a dark-haired beauty who praised his heroic shoulders and square jaw. He would have enjoyed listening to more about his handsome looks. Maybe a few words about his charm. Dreams. Easy come, easy go.

He considered checking on the boys, but that might turn out badly. The creaky floorboards might wake them, or worse, make them think someone was there who shouldn't be. No, he'd wait a bit and see what happens. That's how he approached things when he wasn't sure. Wait and see.

Times like this reminded him that he had no business caring for a ragged bunch of orphaned boys. He'd taken them into his home, not as part of a careful plan, but in the heat of a reckless moment.

Three months ago, he lived alone. Now, six boys slept in the room down the hall. Six young boys.

When he first laid eyes on them, they were shivering and frightened, huddled on the train platform at the Sweet Willow station. The oldest of the group, a youngster in tattered clothes, slipped away from the group, came to his side and begged him for help.

He'd tugged on Noah's sleeve and whispered that he and the others were in a bad way. Could Noah help them?

After a few questions, Noah discovered the ugly truth. The six boys traveled with two men, a despicable pair who intended to take the boys into the mountains to work for the mining company. After a few well-timed blows, Noah sent the men running. They fled Sweet Willow, leaving the boys behind. Noah took the group in. Just for a few nights. That's what he told himself.

That was two months ago.

To his surprise, and everyone else's complete astonishment, the boys worked their way into his hard, cynical heart. Holden was the eldest, twelve years old. He had two brothers, Harold and Hugo. Next came three boys who weren't related, Walt, Dustin and the youngest, a six-year-old by the name of Josiah.

The six boys weren't much trouble. They were so darned grateful for a roof over their head, it made him wonder about what sort of lives they'd led. They even liked his cooking, which was saying something.

The only time they troubled him was in the hours between midnight and dawn. It was in the dead of night when the nightmares came. It seemed that tonight was one of those nights, or so he'd thought when he woke. Now he wasn't so sure.

He scrubbed a hand across his face, trying to figure out what had woken him. The sound that pulled him from his dreams seemed mixed up with the young lady's praise about his fine appearance. A smile tugged at his lips. Truth be told, he prided himself a little on his handsome looks.

"No, make them go away! Mama, make them go away!"

Noah shot from his bed and in an instant was halfway down the hall, stopping in the doorway of the boys' bedroom. Three stacked bunk beds filled the tiny room. Faint moonlight lit the cramped room. He could make out the tousled hair of one of the boys. Dustin. He sat up in bed, shaking with fear.

Noah crossed the room to the bunk. "S'all right, son. It's just a dream."

"Mama?"

Noah patted the boy's shoulder. "Dustin, do I sound like someone's mama?"

"Noah?"

"Yeah, it's me. You're safe. I'm right here."

"The man with the scar across his mouth was trying to get me. He was by the feed store. He was going to take me away."

The feed store – Walt had the same nightmare last week.

Noah spoke gently. "Nobody's taking you anywhere, son. You're in your bed. In your house. And I'm here to make sure no one does anything to hurt you."

The boy sank back to his pillow and replied in a trembling voice. "Okay, Noah."

Noah waited quietly, wondering if the boy would fret any more or drift off to sleep.

When a boy had a nightmare, he'd be all worked up when he woke. When that happened, Noah might spend an hour or more to calm his fears. The terrified boy would insist that the men had returned. They'd come to steal the six boys away and sell them to the mine. And they were right there at the house, lurking in the shadows.

Noah found the best solution was to show them they were safe. He'd light a lamp, take them to the door and show them no one was there. After that, he'd take the boy around the house to check the windows, closets, underneath beds. Sometimes they'd finish and the boy would ask to check everything a second or (Lord help him) a third time. And finally, the boy, exhausted but relieved, would relent and stagger back to bed.

Thank the Lord for small blessings, tonight was not one of those nights. Dustin settled back down without a word. His breathing slowed as he drifted back to sleep. Noah waited by the door to make certain the boy rested.

He eyed the cramped sleeping quarters. Moonlight spilled across the assorted beds and boots. The boys kept the room neat as a pin, but it was still too small for them. The house was meant to be an office for the auction house. It was never meant to be home to a family of seven.

Fortunately, in a few months' time, the family's new house would be finished. The boys wouldn't have to sleep six to a room.

Instead of going back to bed, Noah went to the kitchen to make a pot of coffee.

Anytime one of the boys had a nightmare, Noah could count on being awake for the rest of the night. Their bad dreams always wore him out, but they also left him too restless to sleep. Anger at the men who would sell boys to make a buck grabbed his gut and twisted it. They were a lot like the cattle rustlers he'd helped catch a few years ago. But these men were worse. Far worse.

While nights could be tough, the days were different. He got along well with his band of boys. He managed to clothe, feed and care for all of them, much to his surprise. He took them to church on Sundays, telling them they needed to give thanks to God for what they had. Seeing how they probably never had anything to be thankful for, this was a new idea for them. And he gave them each some daily chores, ones they could do that made them feel useful, which also was new for each of them.

Noah liked to think he was raising them right, but he had his doubts too. At night, when they fretted and called for their mama, he wondered if the whole thing was a mistake. He hated to admit that the boys needed more than he could give.

A week or so after he took them in, he set about finding good homes for them. That ended as quickly as it began. When he explained his plan to find nice families for each of them, the boys saw his good intentions as a betrayal.

All six stared at him with shock and dismay. All of them. And then they fell apart. Even Holden, the twelve-year-old who prided himself on being practically grown, wept that day.

The boys not only hated the idea of a new home, they hated the notion of leaving *his* home. The fear in their eyes caused him to stop talking mid-sentence. He discarded any plans for new homes and promised to keep them. He vowed to never mention the idea again. The boys' gratitude broke his heart, and tears ran down his cheeks for the first time since he was a small boy, hugging the lot of them all at once.

While Noah had no desire for a wife, the boys needed a mama. That was a certainty.

His brother, Seth, had some experience with mail-order brides. Last year, Seth wrote to a matchmaker in Boston, asking if there might be a girl who'd like to come to Texas and become his wife. He told Noah he wanted to start a family, but he didn't have the time or compunction to tramp around Texas looking for one. Noah gave him plenty of grief, laughing and joking that Seth would be lucky to get a woman with ten fingers and hair on her head.

5

Now the shoe was on the other foot, and he regretted poking fun at Seth. Noah recalled all the tormenting he did, like joking that Seth was marrying some stranger, maybe even a disreputable woman. Noah warned him that there was no telling what kind of woman would step off that ship in Galveston.

And then the day came, when the woman from Boston arrived in Galveston, and neither Seth nor Noah could have imagined a lady as sweet and lovely as Laura would be his bride. Now, a year later, Seth was head over boots in love with his wife. Noah had never seen his brother smitten. The man walked around with puppy dog eyes and a dopey smile half the time.

Truth be told, his brother's behavior was a little disconcerting. Seth used to like to play cards and hunt and fish, even fight the neighbor when the wind blew the wrong direction. But now Seth was a changed man, changed for the worse, as far as Noah was concerned. Noah would never get lovesick like that.

Noah didn't want a wife, no sir. While he enjoyed the company of a pretty lady, and they always liked his, that didn't mean he was eager to settle down. He was twenty-five. Old enough, sure, but he always figured he'd stay clear of marriage till he was thirty or so.

In the last two months that notion had changed. It didn't matter what he wanted. Not anymore. He needed to do right by the boys and get himself hitched. A nice, kind-hearted woman who didn't mind he had six youngsters, a gal who had supper waiting and could offer his boys a gentle word.

What he needed was a wife of convenience.

He lit a candle, sat at the table with a mug of coffee, a paper and pen, and began a letter, a letter he never expected to write.

6

Chapter Two

Sarah

Fog and gloom hung over the cemetery, shrouding the trees with a ghostly veil. Headstones stood like grim sentries, sometimes grouped together, like small armies of deceased relatives, sometimes dispersed, like lonely soldiers who never found their way home. Sarah thought the weather was fitting for a funeral.

Otto Becker would have approved... dreary weather for a dreary occasion. The pastor spoke of Otto's life and the blessings he and his wife had brought others. The pastor said nothing about Otto's family, nothing about her. Sarah might have known that her name would not be mentioned.

The funeral had been a hasty affair. There'd been no time to send word to anyone. Her friends and the Beckers' friends would be appalled to find they'd missed the services. It couldn't be helped, however.

Sarah's gaze drifted to Erna's grave. Was it only a month ago that they'd buried her?

Heartache filled her chest. She could hardly imagine life without her Otto and Erna, the sweet couple who had taken her in as a child. She had sparse memories of her own parents who had passed when she was eight.

The day after Otto's passing, a kind gentleman had come to the house to offer his condolences, and to give Sarah an envelope with enough money for her to manage for the next three months. It wasn't much, but it put her mind at ease. The man said that Otto had arranged for the gift outside the will, to not rile any of the blood relatives who would want to lay claim to his meager estate.

Hans Becker, one of Otto's nephews, stood on the other side of the casket, glancing at his watch for a third time. He cleared his throat as if to hurry the service along. Otto and Erna's only blood relative couldn't wait to plunder the contents of the Beckers' tiny home.

The services ended. The few mourners who did come said their farewells and drifted away. They were eager to escape the cold and the damp. Sarah thanked the pastor and turned to leave. Behind her, Hans hurried to catch up. She tried to hasten her step, but alas, he reached her side, stopping her.

"Sarah," Hans said, trying to keep his voice low. "A word?"

"What is it?"

"I wanted to make you aware that I'm not entirely heartless."

"I beg to differ. Your uncle passed away four days ago, yet you've already made plans to sell every stick of furniture. Every book. Every keepsake."

"I'm a businessman, Sarah."

"How much will you get for the little desk Otto built for me for my tenth birthday?" Her voice shook.

"A good sum, actually."

"And the portrait of Erna as a young girl?"

"The portrait, nothing, but the frame is worth a fair bit." His voice held a note of surprise.

Sarah thought of how Erna had cared for her home, her pride in the modest dwelling and her attention to the small details like the pictures. Sarah's melancholy faded to a dull anger. The Beckers had assumed Hans would cherish their belongings. They couldn't have known Hans would sell every single scrap.

The man had no shame.

While Otto was on his deathbed, Hans had come into the home, not to visit his ailing uncle but to make an inventory. He explained that the house didn't belong to Otto and Erna. They'd rented it from him all these years, which came as a shock to Sarah.

He grumbled about the humble furnishings and told her she could take her personal possessions but nothing more. When she asked for a keepsake or two, he erupted, calling her greedy. Ungrateful. Selfish. Hadn't the Beckers done enough for the girl who had once been a filthy orphan?

"You and I should be cordial, at least," Hans said.

"I have nothing to say to you."

"I have something to say to you. Something that might be of interest." He puffed out his chest. "I can offer you work."

"I would *never* work for you."

"You should stay in the shop. You're part of the reason it did so well."

"*Part* of the reason?"

He waved his hand about. "Fine then. A great deal of the reason behind their success."

"I'm leaving San Francisco," she said.

He recoiled. "Where will you go?"

She pulled a letter from her pocket. "I found a letter in Otto's papers. I believe I have a sister. I intend to search for her."

He stared in disbelief. She could see the scorn on his expression. Holding up a gloved hand, she stopped him before he uttered the first word.

"There's nothing for me here. I'm going to look for my sister. I won't stop till I find her."

With that, she turned away. Behind her, Hans sputtered. He called to her, telling her he'd make certain that she would never want for anything. His voice faded in the gloom. She left the cemetery. A soft rain began to fall. Somehow, although she did not like to be out in the rain, the gentle downpour falling on her seemed fitting, and the gathering moisture on her face hid the lines of tears that had fallen from her eyes.

Chapter Three

Noah

Noah found his neighbor, Caleb Walker, near the barn shoeing a horse. As Caleb hammered, sparks sailed through the air. The forge burned bright, sending shimmering waves of heat to the heavens. Noah hung back, not wishing to disturb the man while he worked over a length of red-hot iron.

When Caleb finished, he glanced up. "Hello, Noah, I thought that was you riding up. I didn't see any dogs with you though."

"I've come on a different errand."

Noah shifted his weight from one foot to the other. Both Caleb and Seth had gotten mail-order brides last year, on the same day, in fact. They even arrived on the same boat. Noah was certain the two men would regret getting wives off a boat from Boston, but he was wrong. They were both happily married. Noah had to eat his words.

"Abigail wrote several letters to you before she came to Texas," Noah said, half as a question.

Caleb's expression softened. "That's right. I didn't realize she'd written them. I was writing to the woman she worked for, a Miss Peabody who I've never met, but it turns out Abigail actually wrote most of those letters, and Miss Peabody simply signed them."

"And Abigail ended up arriving on the ship," Noah added.

Caleb's mouth curved into a smile. "That's right. What a day that was."

There was a story. Noah had heard bits of the tale. Abigail had ended up overboard, jumping off the ship to save a child. Caleb jumped into the water to save her and the child. Sopping wet and cold, they introduced themselves to each for the first time in the Port of Galveston. Now they were living in their own happily ever after.

Noah wasn't looking for a happily ever after. Or a wife that made his eyes light like stars. Noah knew better than to believe such fairy tales.

"Since Abigail did such a good job on your letters, I wondered if I could ask her to help me write one of my own."

Caleb's jaw dropped. The horseshoe fell from his tongs, tumbling to the ground. It rolled across the shed and stopped on a sandy patch. Caleb grabbed a pair of thongs, retrieved the horseshoe and rinsed it off in a bucket. He gave Noah a wary look as he returned to his anvil.

"I'm sure she'd be happy to help you."

"I'm much obliged. I know she's busy with the young 'uns. I hate to trouble anyone, especially a new mother."

"My Aunt Eleanor's staying the week. She's here with Doc Whitacre. Your timing is good."

"Heard they got married. Bit of a surprise. All sorts of folks getting married. They're dropping like flies." He chuckled, but his amusement died away.

Caleb frowned. "They happen to be very content. I've never seen my aunt so happy."

"Of course. Marriage can be a good thing," Noah hastened to say. "Or so I've heard from some folks. I'm sure they're telling the truth, for the most part."

12

"They're in the house. Go on in. I'm sure Abigail will be happy to help."

Noah turned and trudged to the house. *Marriage can be a good thing... Like when the woman knows how to cook, and mend, and get up in the middle of the night to soothe a scared boy.*

Caleb hadn't responded to his comment about marriage, probably because the wording was lackluster. Noah had hoped to get a response from Caleb, a yea or nay on the merits of having a wife, but he got nothing except a weak smile. Maybe Caleb knew the truth about marriage, that it was really something to be avoided, when at all possible, but he couldn't say that, could he, what with himself being married and all. Well, Noah wasn't doing it for himself, he had to remind himself. He was doing it for the boys.

He made his way up the wooden steps and knocked on the door. While he waited, he took out his latest attempt at a letter. The tattered paper held more crossed out words than keepers which was why he needed a woman's help.

The sound of thudding echoed across the floor inside. The door opened and Caleb's aunt appeared, a cane in her hand.

Eleanor Walker had, in the last few weeks, become Eleanor Whitacre. In the past, Noah considered her a humorless and severe sort of lady. He noted a change in her expression, a certain liveliness in her eyes.

"Mr. Bailey," she said. "I believe Caleb is in the barn."

"I spoke with him. He said it would be all right if I asked Abigail to help me with something."

"Of course. Please come in. What sort of help?"

"I'm writing a letter, but me and words don't always see eye to eye, if you know what I mean."

"You need help with a letter? What sort of letter?"

"Well, you may have heard I took in a few boys, young'uns. And I like them well enough, but I can't say I always know what to do with them. I intend to take a bride, you see, so the boys have someone to call Mama."

She gave a little gasp. "How lovely!"

"A mail-order bride."

Her smile faltered. "Well. How about that!" She peered at the paper in his hand. "Is that your letter?"

"Yes, ma'am, it is."

He had to admit the scribble-scrabble hardly looked like the type of letter a man might write when he wanted to court a lady. It was the best he could do and that was after several attempts. He wasn't the romantic type, hadn't ever intended to be the romantic type, but he also hadn't intended on being a Papa, and he certainly hadn't planned on having six young'uns, all at once!

Eleanor eyed the letter with clear misgivings. "Abigail can't come just yet. Her babies are both as fussy as can be. Why don't you leave your letter and we'll take a look?"

Noah had been a mite reluctant to write the letter. Now he was impatient to mail it. He didn't relish the notion of waiting even one more day.

"When should I return, ma'am?"

A smile curved her lips. "The eager groom. How delightful."

Eager? Groom? Only one of those words was right. He tried to think of a courteous response that didn't sound like he agreed.

She shook her head. "First thing tomorrow morning. I'll make sure Abigail is up and fresh as a daisy, and then we'll go through your letter and see if it needs anything more."

Reluctantly, he handed over his letter. An unlikely hope came to him. Maybe Abigail would just write the letter for him. Now, wouldn't that be a fine solution. He'd be sure to impress a female if the letter was written by *another* lady. Noah tried to tamp down his enthusiasm for the idea. He bid Eleanor Whitacre a polite farewell and left the Walker Ranch.

Chapter Four

Sarah

In the days following the funeral, Sarah packed her trunks and readied herself to leave her home, the Becker home, and the only city she'd ever known, San Francisco. The work of packing offered a reprieve from her profound grief. Hans insisted she leave the home as soon as possible. Since her train trip was a few days off, she went to stay with her dear friend Victoria Caldicott.

Sarah met Victoria in school, a year after the Beckers had taken her in. Of all her friends, Victoria was the dearest to her, and over the years, Sarah spent so much time in the Caldicott home, Victoria's parents practically viewed her as one of their own.

"This is intolerable." Mr. Caldicott' voice boomed across the dining table. "A young woman, scarcely more than a girl, cannot traipse across the countryside unaccompanied. Don't you agree, dear?"

Mrs. Caldicott smiled demurely. "She's not traipsing, darling. She's going by train."

"To Boston?" he growled, glaring at both Victoria and Sarah. "What do you mean by going all the way across the country, to a strange town, all alone?"

Sarah felt a rush of gratitude toward Mr. Caldicott. His protective manner made her feel cared for and cherished, a comfort to her after being banished from the Becker home.

Victoria gave Sarah a meaningful look from across the table. She mouthed the words, "I told you so."

"Her sister is in Boston." Mrs. Caldicott served her husband another slice of roast beef, adding a dollop of horseradish cream. "Sarah's finally going to meet her sister. Isn't that lovely?"

Mr. Caldicott banged his fist, making his silverware jump. "It's not lovely at all. How can you suggest such a thing?"

"Just imagine if you were in her shoes, darling," Mrs. Caldicott said.

Mr. Caldicott said nothing. He aimed his dark look at his plate and cut into his beef.

"I just received a letter from a woman who knew my sister," Sarah said, trying to soothe Mr. Caldicott' ire. "She's invited me to stay with her."

"I was greatly relieved that Sarah had a place to stay while in Boston," Mrs. Caldicott said. "Especially after the ghastly treatment she received from that young man, the nephew. And if she doesn't find her sister, Sarah will send word. I've promised to send money for a return trip."

"And that sounds to me like more to and fro," Mr. Caldicott grumbled. "I don't like it one bit."

Mrs. Caldicott patted his arm and winked at Sarah.

"Maybe I should go with her," Victoria offered, an impish smile playing on her lips. "Would that make you feel better, Papa?"

"Horsefeathers! I can only imagine what mischief you two girls would get into."

Sarah couldn't help smiling at his outburst. Victoria shrugged a slim shoulder and pouted.

"Who is this lady who wrote you? A respectable type?" Mr. Caldicott demanded.

"I believe so." Sarah took the letter from her pocket. "When I first wrote the orphanage, the director gave my name to a Miss Harriet Peabody. I understand she's now Mrs. Penobscot."

"I don't like it one bit." He gave the envelope another dark, thunderous look.

Sarah gave him the envelope so he could see for himself that she had an acquaintance in Boston. He read it and set it aside. She wasn't sure if it met with his approval or if he'd simply resigned himself to the situation. Over the next few days, both he and Mrs. Caldicott tried to give her extra funds for her trip. Sarah couldn't bear to accept any money, earning her stern lectures from both.

Another letter arrived from Mrs. Penobscot. She recounted a story of Abigail and a mail-order bride agency. She offered few details about Massachusetts Matchmakers, but that couldn't be helped. If her memory served, Abigail might have visited a man by the name of Walker. Mrs. Penobscot felt certain she hadn't stayed in Texas, however. Sarah prayed she'd find clues about her sister in Boston. At the very least, she'd learn more about what might have happened to Abigail.

The day of her departure, Victoria went with her to the train station, despite Sarah's protests.

They stood on the platform, holding hands.

"I'm not crying," Victoria insisted.

"Nor am I."

"I want only to say that I think you're very brave. Far braver than I."

"I will write you as soon as I arrive."

"You had better. And if you don't find your sister, you'll come back to us. Promise me. No need to search everywhere for a long-lost sister. You and I are as close as sisters."

Tears filled Sarah's eyes. Victoria's tender words filled her with bittersweet sadness. She wished she could have lingered a moment or two longer, but the train whistle blasted. The conductor called for the last time. She embraced her dear friend one last time, then turned and boarded the train.

Chapter Five

Holden

As the sun set, Holden hurried to finish hauling water for the ewes and lambs. He paused by the pen, looking from left to right, searching for one of the other boys. Dustin was only eight years old, but he could probably help with his secret task. Or maybe Walt. Definitely not Josiah, the baby of the bunch.

He patted his pocket to assure himself he still had the letter.

A movement caught his attention. The top of Dustin's poky head appeared above the root cellar. Holden whistled low, just loud enough for Dustin to hear. Dustin stuck his head around the corner. When he spotted Holden, he tapped his chest, and Holden nodded and waved him over.

Dustin trotted over, a grin on his grimy face. "Yeah."

"Help me make out what this letter says."

Dustin eyes were wide open. "Where'd you get that?"

"In the fireplace."

The blood drained from Dustin's face. "Oh no... I bet Noah's trying to find a family for me. He's probably tired of me waking him up at night."

"You better stop being a baby. Better stop crying at night."

"I don't mean to, but I get scared. The man grabs me and drags me with him."

"No one's getting dragged nowhere. Noah won't let them."

"Yeah, I guess. But Noah might be tired of me. Just like my g-grandpa."

Holden smacked his shoulder. "Get a hold of yourself. He promised he wouldn't look for a place for any of us, didn't he? Just the same, I want to know what he's writing about."

Dustin let out a deep sigh and rubbed his head. "Can't you read it?"

"Heck, not that chicken scratch. That's why I need your help. You're good at reading. Even messy writing."

Dustin smiled at Holden's praise. He glanced down and knit his brow as he tried to read the letter. "Something about cooking." He scratched his head. "He says us boys are nice and polite."

"Okay, that's good."

Dustin got his worried look all over again. "Not if he's trying to get rid of us."

"Shut up and read. You're fretting like a little girl."

"All right, fine. Let's see. He wrote a bunch of stuff about the auction barn and that his boys could do with a mama."

Holden let out a huff of surprise. Maybe Dustin couldn't read messy handwriting after all. Holden expected Dustin to admit he'd made a mistake. That the letter said something entirely different. But Dustin didn't say anything about a mistake. Instead, he kept on with the same nonsense.

"It says something about getting a nice lady," Dustin said.

"Now I know you're lying."

"Not either. That's what it says right here," he said, pointing at the page. "What's wrong with a nice lady?"

Holden chuckled. He'd intended to show he didn't believe a word, but the laugh came out a little rusty. "Not a thing. The only trouble is Noah isn't courting. How's he supposed to get a mama for us boys if he doesn't even talk to any ladies? We

22

don't have any to choose from in Sweet Willow. None that want a fella with six kids. He's told me just that."

Dustin shrugged. He went back to reading the letter, moving his lips as he progressed. "It doesn't say how he's going to get a mama. Just that it might be a good idea."

Holden rolled his eyes. "You're not reading it right. I reckon all this is for nothing. Don't tell the others that Noah's taken up writing letters. They'll just carry on about him giving us to some family and that's not what this is about."

"Sure. If you say so."

Dustin scratched his head again. Seemed the boy still had bugs like they all did when Noah took them in. Holden hoped that wasn't the case. It would mean another dose of that bad-smelling head scrub, three days in a row. And they'd have to wash their bed linens too.

He frowned at Dustin. "Gimme that letter. I need to put it back in the fireplace."

"You shouldn't be taking Noah's stuff. Seems wrong."

"Really? Thank you kindly for today's mighty fine sermon, Pastor Dustin."

Holden stuffed the letter in his pocket and returned to finishing up the last of his chores. While he worked, he kept wondering why in the world Noah would be writing so many letters, and what he was doing, and why was he throwing so many of them away?

Noah better not have changed his mind about keeping them, Holden thought. There was nothing worse than a grown up going back on his word. And Holden should know... he'd seen plenty of that already.

He filled his last bucket of water and hauled it to the sheep pen. The water sloshed against his leg. He hardly noticed the cold. Instead, he considered what he'd do if he found more discarded, rumpled letters. One thing he knew for certain. Next time he needed help with Noah's messy writing, he'd ask someone other than Dustin to help him make sense of it.

Chapter Six

Noah

After breakfast, Noah left the boys with instructions to do their chores and mind their manners. He'd better not hear a bunch of sad, tearful tales of bickering or scuffles or other trouble they might rustle up. Any questions went to Holden, the man in charge. Holden seemed to like being the leader. Anytime Noah left him in charge of things, he kept order like it was a matter of personal pride.

Noah rode to the Walker ranch, praying that Abigail would have time to help him. Shoot, maybe she'd already rewritten the letter and made it romantic and gentlemanly, the way it should be. The main thing was, he needed a letter he could send, today. He felt quite pleased, thinking the letter would be there on the dining table, ready for him to sign and slip into the scented envelope.

Then his concerns grabbed him. What if her babies still fussed, or Abigail hadn't had the energy to read his letter, or Mrs. Whitacre hadn't even shown her the letter yet? He realized he was being foolish, his hopes and fears jumping back and forth across his thoughts while he rode, but this was important business, and urgent. The next few days he'd be busy with a yearling auction. If she couldn't spare a few moments now, he'd have to wait a whole week to try again.

What he really wanted was to set this tomfoolery out of his mind and get back to important matters. And to sleep the night through again, every night, with a mama to care for the boys when they had their bad dreams.

He made the trip quickly, needing to know if the letter was ready. When he arrived, he hopped off the horse and tied it to the hitching post, then quickly jumped up the steps and knocked on the front door. When he heard someone approach, he snatched his hat from his head and raked his fingers through his hair. Had he combed it before he left? Hard to say.

There had been a time when he'd dress with care before paying a visit. Not anymore. Nowadays he barely remembered to drag a razor across his whiskers. Aside from going to Church on Sundays, he hardly ever thought about his attire. The boys brought about this change. Just as soon as he took them in, his dapper ways fell by the wayside.

Caleb's aunt opened the door. "Good morning, Romeo."

Sparks of amusement danced in Eleanor's eyes as she drew the door back and ushered him inside. His face warmed with embarrassment. She'd read his letter and found it lacking. He felt a mix of irritation and relief. His letter wasn't good. But at least Abigail might be able to help. Maybe Eleanor too. At this point, he didn't care who wrote the letter.

Eleanor showed him to the parlor. Her skirts rustled as she left, a smile still playing upon her lips. A moment later Abigail arrived.

"I'm sorry to impose, Mrs. Walker."

"Please call me Abigail." Lifting her hands to her hair, she smoothed a few loose strands. "I'm in a bit of a disarray. I was up in the night with one of the boys."

A servant entered the parlor, holding a toddler by the hand. "Mama," the boy whimpered. He held out a hand, straining against the servant's firm grasp.

"I'm sorry, Mrs. Walker. He heard your voice and insisted on seeing you."

Abigail gave a weary smile. "That's fine, Dorothy. Let him go. I've missed my boy this morning while I was busy with the babies."

The boy pulled away from the servant and toddled towards Abigail, his arms outstretched. Abigail lifted him and kissed him, wrapping him in a warm embrace. "My great big boy. Can you be a little angel while I talk with Mr. Bailey?"

The boy nodded and rested his head on her shoulder.

"With some luck I'll get him to take a you-know-what," Abigail murmured. "Do you mind, Mr. Bailey?"

"No, ma'am. Please call me Noah."

Abigail settled on the chesterfield with the boy in her arms. The little one nestled closer and stuck his thumb in his mouth. She gestured for Noah to sit on a nearby chair.

"Someone's tired," she said softly, stroking the boy's head. "Hopefully."

Noah felt overcome with awkwardness, disliking the position he found himself in. He didn't want to trouble anyone, especially a busy mother of three very small children. He was smack in the middle of a quandary. Plain and simple. But it couldn't be helped.

With a sigh, he began to explain. "After a half-dozen tries, I've gotten a start on a letter, but you probably noticed I could use a few pointers. So far, I managed to explain all about the auction house, which is interesting, but I haven't said much about other things."

Abigail managed to keep her hold on the boy and glance at the nearby table. His letter sat beside paper and pen. She winced and returned her attention to him.

"Yes, I read your letter last night."

He couldn't tell what she thought. Shifting on the edge of his chair, he tugged at his collar. He kept his voice low so as not to disturb the child. "Think I ought to add a little more about the hog sales on the first Thursday of the month?"

"Well..." She laughed softly, as she took the letter and studied the contents.

"I could talk about the new goat pens."

"Goat pens?"

"I aim to make Bailey Auction Barn the finest outfit in South Texas. She might like to know about my plans."

"I didn't realize you wanted to get married, Noah. When did this come about?"

"A few months back I took in some youngsters. I'm guessing you know about that."

Abigail nodded, but seemed to be more focused on soothing her child than what Noah was saying.

"Well, I've had some trouble finding any help and would like to have a lady to cook for us. That's my main concern – finding a cook who can give the boys a little tenderness. There aren't too many women in Sweet Willow who want a man with a family. Then there's the matter of my reputation."

"A matter of your reputation?" Abigail's tone held a note of concern. The boy squirmed in her arms and grumbled sleepily. Abigail kissed his forehead. "There, there, my sweet boy."

"Reputation?" a woman's voice echoed from the hallway. Eleanor came into the parlor, an expression of curiosity written clearly on her features. She took a seat beside Abigail. "Don't mind me. I'm just eavesdropping."

The boy fidgeted and sat up. Seeing Eleanor, he clambered down from Abigail's lap. He went to Eleanor, who wrapped him in her arms and patted his back. In an instant the boy had closed his eyes and gone back to sleep.

"You're spoiling this child," Eleanor said softly, giving Abigail a look of mild rebuke. "He's made up his mind that he can't nap unless he's rocked to sleep."

Abigail went on, glancing from the letter to Noah and back again. "The main thing you want is someone to cook meals for you and the boys. Is that right?"

"Yes, ma'am."

Eleanor made a sound, a sort of muffled snort. Eleanor might be happily married, but she probably wasn't spending her days over a stove. She likely had servants for every task she could think of and then a few more.

Abigail went on. "Perhaps we should add a few more words about cooking abilities."

"Sounds fine. A wife ought to know her way around the kitchen. I'm a big eater. So are the boys. Pretty sure they all got hollow legs."

Abigail leaned forward, tilting her head slightly. "What boys?"

Noah frowned. "I'm sorry. That's what I meant by the youngsters I took in."

Abigail rubbed her temples. "I'm sorry. You just said that. I'd already forgotten. I'm so tired today, I don't know if I'm coming or going." She shook her head and smiled. "I've been so busy with *my* boys. Tell me about the youngsters. I want to know how this came about. I confess that the notion of you raising children, by yourself, comes as a surprise."

"That's what everyone says."

Noah braced himself for what might end up being yet another lecture about parenting. Anytime he spoke of the boys, he'd get an earful. If it wasn't Mrs. Finch outside the bakery listing off proper breakfasts for growing boys, it was Mr. Carlyle at the mercantile insisting Noah shouldn't let the boys have a stick of candy after Saturday shopping.

Folks griped about the boys working in the auction house. Those people liked to go on about him taking advantage. Then there were others who claimed he wasn't working the boys enough. They'd catch wind of him letting his boys spend a Saturday afternoon at the swimming hole. He was spoiling them. Clearly. They'd grumble. The band of orphans was sure to grow up to be a bunch of ne'er-do-wells.

No matter what he did, there were those who liked to point out it was wrong. The good people of Sweet Willow could agree on one thing. Noah Bailey had no business taking in a half-dozen motherless boys.

With a sigh, he began his tale. "Well, a few months ago, right around the time I opened the auction house, I had to go to the train station. I saw a fella with a passel of young boys. They acted pretty skittish. Fearful. Come to find out they'd been picked up by a couple of mining scouts."

"Mining scouts?"

"That's right. A disreputable bunch. They work the smaller towns around here looking for boys who are on their own. Orphans, for the most part. They make all sorts of promises to the boys. They say they know of families who want a boy to love. It's nothing but lies. They take them into the mountains west of here. They force them into jobs nobody wants. The mining operations hire kids there so they can pay them less than they pay the grown men. Which isn't a lot. And they pay a bounty for each boy."

Eleanor shook her head, her eyes lighting with indignation.

Abigail grew pale. She folded the letter and set it aside. "I see. So you'd like your wife to cook for you and the boys?"

"That's right, all seven of us."

The two ladies stared. Silence stretched between them, making Noah feel a prickle of discomfort. Neither of the ladies spoke. What was so darned curious about wanting supper at night, he'd like to know.

"Can we talk about the pens in the auction yard a little more?" he asked.

"There are *seven* of you?" Abigail asked, her voice faint.

"Yes, ma'am."

"Your bride will take on marriage and six boys," Abigail murmured. "Seven menfolk under one roof."

"Well. Yes." He shrugged. "Seven of us."

Eleanor's brows lifted as her mouth curved into a smile. She leaned forward, careful not to disturb the sleeping boy. "I'm going to call your bride Snow White."

Abigail said nothing. Her jaw hung slightly slack and she kept her gaze fixed on him as if she expected him to tell her he was only joking.

"Maybe it would be best to put that in the letter," Noah offered. "The part about the six boys. Probably would be bad to surprise her with that sort of thing."

"Probably," Eleanor murmured, smiling sweetly. "I'd imagine she might be surprised. Not everyone likes surprises unless they come in small, velvet boxes."

He could say the same for himself. He didn't much care for surprises. What if his bride turned out to be a woman twenty years his senior with a bunch of her own kids in tow? He'd prefer she not arrive in the family way either, but how could he explain something like that to a couple of refined ladies?

Not that he didn't care for children. Heck, he'd taken in a slew of them.

"I don't want for either of us to be surprised," he said, hoping his meaning was clear.

"Six boys." Eleanor chuckled. "I wonder if your boys had anything to do with the teacher quitting the Sweet Willow School." She waved a dismissive hand. "Listen to me. I'm sure they're good as gold. Your bride is going to fall in love with the lot of you."

Fall in love? That idea hadn't crossed his mind. He dwelled on a sweet, loving bride for a moment. He pushed the idea away and considered Eleanor's words about the teacher quitting.

He'd taken the boys in a little better than two months ago. They'd attended the Sweet Willow School for the couple of weeks of school and yes, the teacher had up and quit, but he hadn't suspected his boys had anything to do with her departure. It had to be purely coincidental. Surely.

They were fond of pranks. That much was true. But that lady probably had somewhere to go in a hurry. That must have been why she'd taken the first train out of Sweet Willow the last day of school.

He pushed the worry aside. The most important thing was corralling a mama for the boys. She could take care of any teacher trouble. He made a mental note to request a wife before school started up again.

"I don't really know anything about the teacher quitting, ma'am," Noah said.

Eleanor nodded. "Of course. Maybe she gave up her position to spend more time with her family."

Noah noted a slight hint of amusement in her tone. Her expression remained solemn, however, so he couldn't be sure. Some ladies were hard to figure out. All ladies were trouble in that way. Why couldn't they just be simple like menfolk, he wondered.

"I never intended any of this," he said. "When I saw those boys at the train station, I acted without thinking. Later, after I got them settled, I thought about finding homes for them here in Sweet Willow, but I couldn't bring myself to send them away."

"That's so kind of you, Noah," Eleanor said the words softly.

"They're rascals. All of them. But each of them is like a little..." He stopped himself, feeling utterly foolish.

The ladies sat quietly, listening intently.

He went on, suddenly unconcerned with how he sounded. "I don't know the first thing about children. But these boys seem like little jigsaw puzzles. You know? Each has a piece or two missing. Maybe a piece that's broken. Seth and me grew up in a loving home. So I can't really know what these boys have been through. And maybe I don't want to know. In the beginning, some of them took extra food and hid it away, like they might not get another meal any time soon. That's just plain wrong."

Abigail's eyes shone. She pressed her lips together and averted her gaze. Maybe that was a sign for him to hush, but he forged on.

"And the other day I sorta yelled at Walt. Didn't mean to do it but how many times do I need to explain about shutting the gate? I can't risk horses getting loose. So I might have hollered. A little. Come suppertime, I couldn't find the boy anywhere. Took me two hours of searching. I was about to ride over to the sheriff to round up a search party."

"You found him, I presume?" Eleanor said.

"Hiding under his bed. Curled up into a ball. Scared half out of his wits."

Neither lady spoke.

Noah raked his hand through his hair. "He scared me half out of my wits too. So you can see why I'd do better with a feminine influence."

"Indeed," said Eleanor.

Abigail took a pad and pen from a nearby table and began to write. "Well, Noah, let's not speak of bygones. I shall add to your words. Between the two of us, we'll pen the perfect letter. For the sake of those sweet boys."

He didn't miss the way her hand trembled.

"Sorry to tell you all that," he said quietly.

Abigail glanced up from the paper and offered Noah a smile. "A mama for the boys and a wife for you. We need a few words about cooking and a few more about romance and devotion."

Noah felt a twinge in his shoulder, likely from sitting so long in the company of ladies. Nothing about the visit was going as he had imagined. He wished it could have been avoided altogether. He certainly didn't want to confess that he needed a wife in name only. A simple marriage of convenience. He'd make a note to add that part in before mailing the letter.

He would have rather been riding the pastures. Or getting ready for a cattle sale. Or anything other than listening to women talk about romance and devotion. He resolved to stay quiet and keep his thoughts to himself. If he was going to be living with a woman soon, it was probably best he start practicing that sort of thing anyway.

Chapter Seven

Sarah

The journey to Boston cost Sarah most of her meager savings. She'd intended to go to Mrs. Penobscot first thing. Instead, she asked the driver of the hansom cab to take her to Massachusetts Matchmakers and her trunks to the home of Mrs. Penobscot.

Waiting in the agency's foyer, she drew her shawl closer and fought a growing desperation. A cold Boston wind blew down the chimney. The fire in the hearth glowed and flickered from the gust of air. She tapped her foot nervously.

A sign hung on the wall. *We Specialize in Love and Forevermore.*

Sarah shifted on the sagging chesterfield.

The agency's secretary glanced up a time or two, pursing her lips with clear disdain.

For two hours, Sarah waited. During that time, she saw a half-dozen young women or more trailing into the office of the matchmaker. Some were dressed in fine clothes, obviously wealthy. Others wore threadbare frocks and scuffed, ragged boots.

Sarah pitied the girls who ventured into the small agency, daring to wear old dresses. Those dressed in tattered frocks, without exception, fled the small office with tear-filled eyes.

Her gaze drifted to another sign near the door. *We Promise an Adventure in Wedded Bliss*

Wedded bliss? The girls who'd left in tears might have a different opinion. It was clear the agency only wanted clients of a certain class. Perhaps they sought beautiful girls too. Although Sarah couldn't imagine becoming a mail-order bride, she wondered if a man might find her pretty.

Otto and Erna always told her she was lovely. Otto used to call her his angel eyes, even as his own sight faded and eventually failed him. And Erna bragged on Sarah's pretty hair, especially when she wore it loose, a cascade of blonde curls that tumbled past her shoulders.

The door opened. A gentleman filled the doorframe, frowning at her as if she were no more than a speck of lint on his fine wool suit.

"I thought I'd seen all the applicants for the day."

"That one wants to know about her sister, Mr. Perryman," the secretary muttered. "Been here an hour or more."

"My name is Sarah Becker, sir." She got to her feet and smiled shyly. He eyed her as if she were a slab of meat displayed in a butcher's window. Would he make her cry as he had the others?

"Pretty." His brows lifted. "You're not interested in becoming a mail-order bride?"

"I hoped you might be able to help me find my sister. I understand she traveled to Galveston to meet a man by the name of Walker."

"I can't help you find a person. Not unless it's a husband." He drew his brows together. "Are you sure you don't want to become a mail-order bride?"

"I might be interested." She schooled her features to look earnest. She wasn't entirely against the idea of becoming a mail-order bride. She wasn't against the idea of becoming a streetsweeper for that matter. Which might be a consideration when the last of her money ran out. She couldn't impose on Mrs. Penobscot for more than a day or two.

"Well, at least you look as though you'd fit some of my requests. Not like the other riff-raff that's come through my door today. Come in. Let's see if you're the sort of girl my clients ask about. You don't have children, do you?"

He turned and went back inside his office. Sarah hurried after him. While she wasn't interested in what he offered, she had to at least play along.

"No children. I've never been married."

Sitting down heavily behind his desk, Mr. Perryman scoffed. "Neither have half the other girls who come seeking husbands. That didn't stop them from having a few brats along the way."

She shook her head. "I do not have any children."

"References?"

"From San Francisco."

He rolled his eyes and leaned back in his chair. "Are you a good cook?"

Sarah coaxed her lips into a smile. "Of course."

Which was not quite a lie. Not really. It wasn't quite the truth either.

Mr. Perryman, she presumed, wanted to know if she could cook savory roasts, baked chicken, soups and stews. She'd never cooked those dishes. She *did* know how to make candies and sweet treats, the finest in San Francisco.

Customers who patronized Otto and Erna's sweet shop raved about her chocolate sauce and the cream-filled cakes she created. Her truffles inspired one devoted customer to write poetry. Shoppers ordered Christmas cakes in May and

39

her raspberry drops sold out each morning moments after the shop opened its doors.

She was the reason the little shop was famous, which was why Hans was so eager to keep her on. Sweets and candies were her claim to fame. Not Beef Wellington or Chicken Divan. She knew what he meant when he asked if she could cook, but she chose not to explain. After all, she was here to find out about her long-lost sister, mot to discuss cooking skills.

Mr. Perryman grumbled under his breath. "The pretty, nicely dressed ones don't know how to do a thing. The worn, shabbily dressed ones can cook but aren't the type my clients want to marry." He sighed. "It's not easy. I never have enough nice girls to keep up with requests."

"Terribly sorry, but the reason I've come is to inquire about my sister."

"And the ones that cook curse like sailors."

"Shocking. I'm sure your work is a trial. My sister's name is Abigail Winthrop."

"So why is your last name Becker?" Suspicion darkened his eyes. "I thought you said you weren't married."

"The Winthrops, my parents, died when I was a child. I was adopted by an elderly Austrian couple. The Beckers."

"And where are they?"

"They passed away."

He smiled, a greedy spark lighting his eye. "You're wearing a pretty frock and look like an upstanding young lady. Tell me, did they leave you a fortune?"

"No." Sarah's voice caught. "They did not."

"That's a shame." He rocked back in his chair and clasped his hands behind his back. His vest stretched taut across his barrel chest. He gave her an appreciative glance that made her skin prickle. "My, but you're a comely girl. I could raise my fees if I had more like you. I have a boat leaving in a few weeks."

Sarah shivered. She'd never been entirely comfortable around big, strapping men, particularly if they were strangers. She was grateful that a broad desk stood between them.

"My main concern is to find my sister."

He tapped his fingers on his desk. "I could pay your way to Texas. After you get there, you could look for your sister."

Tempting. So tempting. But she'd just finished a long, long voyage. Endless train rides. Bumpy and dusty carriage rides. Delays. Snoring travel companions. An unfortunate two-day trip on the back of a cart drawn by a bad-tempered mule.

It was the mule that had been the final straw.

When she arrived in Boston that morning, Sarah hoped to never step foot on another train. A journey by ship didn't sound appealing either. Before embarking on any sort of journey to Texas, she'd need to make absolutely certain Abigail was in Texas.

"No, thank you. I'd prefer to write her first, if only you'd help me find her. Your secretary said you might know."

"I should fire that chit. I don't have records of prior clients. I happen to have a gentleman client in Sweet Willow," he said.

Sarah's heart thudded.

"That sounds intriguing." She winced at her clumsy ploy. "Is he a decent sort of gentleman? A good Christian man?"

Mr. Perryman held up a letter and waved it back and forth. "The finest gentleman I've ever had the pleasure of doing business with. He's a banker. An elderly man, but well-established in town."

Sarah schooled her features to keep from showing her distaste. Marrying a stranger? How could a woman bring herself to exchange vows with a man she didn't know?

"Would you like to read his letters? I would allow you to take them home if you promised to return them tomorrow first thing. The man is very rich and owns several banks in South Texas. Three houses too. He's eager to marry again. Did I mention he's rich?"

If she refused to at least take the letters, that would be the end of the discussion. She'd have to leave empty-handed. With a sinking heart, she realized that even if she discovered Abigail was indeed in Texas, it would be near impossible to make the trip any time soon. She had almost no money.

Sarah took the letters and turned them over in her hand. The man's handwriting looked tidy. She pictured a kindly man. A noble man. Her mind filled with girlish imaginings. A plan formed in her mind. What if she could find a devoted husband in Sweet Willow? She could have a home near her long-lost sister...

"You'd best be sure you don't have children," Mr. Perryman growled. "The fellow in this letter has been married three times and has eleven of his own."

Sarah almost dropped the bundle of letters. "Just eleven?"

"Very funny." He scowled. "Take the letters. Read them. Meantime, I'll look through my ledger and see if I can find anything about your sister. Here, take a few more letters. I have one from a merchant in Houston. A saddler in San Antonio and a fellow who owns an auction house in Sweet Willow. You might like that fellow since he might know of your sister."

His tone suggested the conversation was over. He went back to sorting his papers.

Sarah gazed at the letters with regret. Why had she agreed to read them? She reminded herself of her yearning to find Abigail as she held the bundle of letters from the banker gentleman. Eleven children! Three prior wives! What had happened to the poor women, Sarah wondered. With a heavy sigh, she tucked the letters in her pocketbook and showed herself out.

Chapter Eight

Noah

Whenever Noah woke in the predawn darkness, his thoughts often turned to self-betterment. He knew he was a selfish man. He also knew he was blind to a great deal of his self-centered ways. His shortcomings had never been so plain in the last few months since he took the boys in.

When he first discovered the group of boys waiting at the train station along with the man posing as their caretaker, Noah didn't hesitate to act.

In that instant, Noah had acted unselfishly. It wasn't his custom. He preferred to lead his life in a simple but admittedly self-interested way. He didn't bother others. He expected the same in return.

Take Sunday services, for example. In the past, he often went long spells without attending. For the past four months, eighteen weeks if you counted (which he did), he'd attended church every Sunday morning. Eighteen straight. Why, he probably hadn't been to eighteen services in the past five years.

And each Sunday morning, when he found himself awake, staring into the darkness, he imagined how pleasant it would be to stay put. His bed was warm. Comfortable. He could just close his eyes and slip back into sleep. The boys wouldn't complain. Heck, they'd probably do cartwheels across the auction house courtyard to celebrate.

Maybe not Josiah. Noah groaned, thinking about the boy.

The youngest loved church and claimed he intended to be a preacher one day. But the rest of them would hoot and holler. Right after that, they'd clamor for breakfast. Land sakes, the boys could eat. Like a bunch of locusts passing through.

He groaned and got out of bed, saying a hasty prayer before washing and dressing.

And then began the process of waking the boys, telling them to get dressed in church clothes, feeding them and loading them onto the buckboard. By the time he reached the Sweet Willow Church, he'd already said a dozen prayers. He wasn't entirely sure if prayers counted if the person grumbled while praying to the Almighty, but he said them anyway, if for no other reason than to prevent him from saying other things that were on his mind.

He supposed God looked down upon his prayers favorably, because an hour later, there they were. All seven of them, taking up the last pew in church. What was it about putting on respectable clothes that made the boys squabble? When they wore their dungarees, they didn't fuss.

"Morning, Noah," said a neighbor.

"Nice to see you," said another.

"You made it!" cheered a young couple.

Noah managed a wan smile, noting their surprise. Most everyone in Sweet Willow regarded him with that same surprise ever since he'd taken on the six shooters.

He sighed, feeling tired. He'd indicated in his letter to the matchmaking agency that he'd like a bride sooner rather than later. Despite Abigail's kind help, the letter probably came across as desperate because, well, he *was* desperate. He'd scarcely introduced himself and already he was practically begging for them to send a girl.

Dr. Whitacre and Eleanor strolled past and took a seat near the front. Noah kept his weary gaze fixed on her elegant hat throughout the services. She seemed so refined. So different than the women in Sweet Willow.

After the service, she found him outside the church. Her eyes lit with curiosity. Standing on the top of the church stairs, she called to him and waved. When she spied the boys, she smiled, her eyes lighting with amusement. She said a few words to Dr. Whitacre and made her way through the crowd.

Noah groaned.

As he studied his troop of boys, they seemed to his thinking to appear more disheveled than usual. More raggedy. It didn't make sense, really. He'd bought each boy two sets of Sunday clothes a few days after they came to live with him.

They'd gone to the tailor in Sweet Willow, spending half the day to get fitted. Holden and his two brothers had managed the day without much problem, having lived some years with an elderly couple who'd been duped into sending them to work at Sierra Mine.

Dustin, Walt and Josiah had been another matter entirely. They'd drifted plenty over the course of their childhood, from various homes to orphanages. Not one of them had ever had a new set of clothing. Every article of clothing they owned was threadbare and moth-eaten. Their boots were worn almost clear through.

Getting them fitted into something decent had been like trying to herd a passel of greased roadrunners. They'd squirmed and complained, and one of them, Walt maybe, had darted out of the tailor's shop a half-dozen times. He quit after Noah threatened to lasso him.

As they stood outside the church, Noah considered his motley pack of boys and how they must look to a fancy lady like Eleanor Walker. Their garments were neat enough, if not pressed perfectly, or pressed at all if the truth were told, not since the last laundry lady had up and quit.

The boys shifted from foot to foot, clearly uncomfortable under Eleanor's studious gaze. Somehow, they managed to look more ragtag than when he first saw them huddled on the Sweet Willow train platform.

Walt, who had an aversion to combs, had also misbuttoned his shirt. How could a ten-year-old miss not one button, but two? The oversight naturally made tucking his shirt in problematic, if not impossible.

And Harold, who usually was the careful one in the group, wore a shirt that clearly belonged to a younger boy. The sleeves barely came halfway down his forearms. Not one of the boys had both shoes tied. Walt's shoes were not only untied but on the wrong feet.

He pinched the bridge of his nose and braced himself before turning to face Eleanor.

"Please introduce me to these nice-looking youngsters, won't you?" she asked as she pulled on a pair of gloves.

"Yes, ma'am." He went through the line, listing off names. "Holden, the eldest, his brothers Harold and Hugo. Dustin with the freckles. Walton, or Walt, who forgot to use his comb this morning – sorry about that, and the youngest, Josiah."

To his surprise, she regarded the boys with misty eyes. For a long moment, she said nothing. Her hand drifted to her lips. After a slow, trembling breath, she let her hand fall.

"You're doing a fine thing, Noah," she said quietly.

"Thank you."

He tugged at his collar and hoped she wasn't about to weep for some reason. He could hardly stand a woman's tears. They tore at his heart more than anything. His brother, Seth, had adopted a girl, Francine, or Frankie as she liked to be called. Noah loved the girl something fierce but could hardly be in the same room as her anytime she got to crying. Ever since he'd taken in the boys, she'd cried plenty. The girl seemed to feel slighted. She couldn't stand the boys, refusing to call them by their names but referring to them as a group – The Sweet Willow Pests.

Her eyes teared up anytime he came around Seth's ranch with one of his little tagalongs.

Thank the good Lord for boys. Oh, there might be a little sniffling here and there, but nothing like a female.

Thankfully, Eleanor held her tears back. She lifted her chin as if trying to regain her dignity.

"You'd think we don't have mirrors at our place," Noah said, trying to change the subject for Eleanor's sake. "These boys aren't old enough yet to try to catch a girl's eye."

Eleanor laughed. "Not yet. It'll be here before you know it. Time goes by faster than you can imagine."

Her voice faltered. Noah fretted that she might tear up again. She recovered, however.

"What you need is a helpmeet," Eleanor said, patting him on the shoulder. "So you don't have to do it all by yourself."

"Yes, ma'am." He gave her a lopsided grin. "That's exactly what I need. Someone who can lend a hand. I'm gruff and short-tempered. They all need tender loving care. The kind that only a woman can provide."

"I'm praying for you, Noah. I hope she gets here soon." Eleanor turned away, pausing before she left as a smile played upon her lips. "Godspeed, Snow White."

Chapter Nine

Sarah

Harriet Penobscot welcomed Sarah into her home with open arms. Harriet's warm greeting came as a great relief after her ordeal at the matchmaking agency. Harriet met her at the door with an embrace, almost knocking Sarah over.

Harriet took her inside and showed her to the guest quarters, talking excitedly about how surprised and pleased she was that Sarah had come all the way to Boston.

"It's lovely to meet you and to have company. My Reginald is away. I get a little lonesome without him." Harriet's hand drifted to her waist. "Especially with a little one on the way."

"And it's lovely to meet you. Thank you for your kind hospitality."

Harriet waved a dismissive hand and told one of the servants to bring tea and refreshments for Miss Becker. Then she set about helping Sarah unpack her trunk. Harriet fussed over her. She asked a dozen questions about Sarah's life in San Francisco.

Sarah sipped tea as she set her things in the wardrobe. She recounted what she knew, which wasn't very much. Her parents had left Abigail behind. They'd intended to come back for her. Sarah wasn't certain how they'd died. Both had become ill and passed within days of each other.

That evening over supper, Harriet marveled how very much Sarah resembled Abigail.

"You favor each other. You even have the same mannerisms."

Sarah blushed. "I've scarcely come to terms that I have a sister. It's nice to know that we might favor each other."

Harriet's eyes shone as if she might shed a tear. "I miss Abigail. She was a good friend to me. I'm happily married, but a husband's company is not the same as the friendship between women."

Sarah agreed. Aside from Victoria, she'd left behind several dear friends in San Francisco. As the evening wore on, it became clear to her that Abigail must not have returned from Texas. Harriet insisted that if Abigail had returned, she would have heard the news.

After dinner, they strolled in the gardens behind the house. Paths wound past fountains and carefully tended flowerbeds. The last rays of evening sun cast golden light across the blooms and hedges.

Harriet sighed. "I'm under strict orders to take a walk each evening and to avoid sweets."

"From your doctor?"

Harriet rolled her eyes. "Yes, and from my dear Reginald. He's just as bad."

Sarah smiled and resolved not to mention the Beckers' sweet shop. Better not to talk of tempting sweets. The memory of the small store seemed distant and shrouded in haze. It felt like years since she'd worked there instead of only two months.

Harriet slipped her arm through Sarah's. "I'm afraid I must give you a confession."

Sarah waited, wondering what on earth Harriet would need to confess.

"Before I married my dear Reginald, I had intended to travel to Texas as a mail-order bride. I planned to marry Mr. Walker."

Sarah drew a sharp breath.

"My circumstances changed." Harriet's voice faltered. "In the end, Abigail went in my place."

"I see."

Harriet winced. "I left the ship hastily, before it set sail. Abigail remained on board."

"Did she know you'd gotten off?"

"That's the thing, you see." Harriet bit her lip before going on. "I left her a note. She must not have found it before the ship set sail."

They walked in silence. A cool, early summer breeze carried the scent of roses. Sarah's mind hummed with so many thoughts, it was hard to know what to fix her mind upon. Abigail had left Boston. Alone. To travel to a distant shore to meet a man. A stranger.

Harriet let out a trembling sigh. "You must hate me."

Before Sarah could say that she was wrong, Harriet went on.

"You can't hate me as much as I hate myself."

"I don't hate you. Not in the least."

"My fervent hope is that Abigail is well. Perhaps she and Mr. Walker met and fancied each other. That sort of thing happens to mail-order brides. Some are very happy, so I've heard."

Harriet's voice shook with anguish. Sarah patted her hand. To change the subject, she spoke of her visit with the matchmaker. They walked along a path that headed back to the house. Harriet seemed fatigued but smiled at Sarah's tales of Mr. Perryman.

"He insisted he could find me a husband."

"I'm sure he would love to send a pretty girl like you to one of his lonely bachelors." Harriet smiled. "But I shall try to convince you to stay in Boston."

"What? And miss wedded bliss with a seventy-year-old grandfather?"

"Oh, dear. He didn't really want to marry you off to an elderly man?"

"He did indeed. I have a few more letters from prospective grooms. I wonder how many have their own teeth?"

Harriet laughed until her eyes shone with tears. "They probably want a nursemaid. Someone to cut their food into small bites."

"That was my thinking too. Perhaps I should practice speaking to the aged."

"How would you do that?"

"By shouting," Sarah said in a booming voice. "I said, by shouting! And repeating myself!"

They returned to the house. Harriet begged to see the letters from the agency. She playfully suggested that she had just the sort of experience needed to pick out the perfect match. They spent the next hour reading through the elderly banker's letters.

He'd written at length about his requirements for a quiet, docile wife. One who knew her place and always greeted him with a smile.

Harriet gave Sarah a look of mocking concern. "He's mentioned his slippers three times now. His wife should meet him at the door, at the end of the day, remove his boots and *lovingly* put his slippers on his feet."

Sarah stood by the fireplace, enjoying the warmth of the cheerful blaze. "How delightful. Does he say he'll do the same for his poor, long-suffering wife?"

Harriet sorted through the papers. "Doesn't say anything about him offering to tend to his wife, I'm afraid."

Sarah waved a dismissive hand. "Next gentleman, if you please."

"Let's see. We decided the saddler in San Antonio wouldn't do. His home is over the livery barn." Harriet wrinkled her nose. "The merchant in Houston is problematic."

"How so? Does he live over a barn as well?"

"No barn." Harriet scanned the letter. "But from his letter, I suspect the merchant is actually a butcher."

"What's wrong with that?" Sarah asked with idle curiosity. She had no intention of actually going through with the mail-order charade, but still, she enjoyed discussing the various men.

Harriet grumbled. "The smell might be worse than the livery barn."

Sarah marveled at the notion of marrying a stranger. Had her sister married the gentleman in Texas? If so, was she happy? Sarah liked to think so. Thoughts of Abigail were bittersweet. On one hand, her heart thrilled to know she had a sister. On the other hand, she'd come all this way, probably for nothing.

"What about the last letter? The fellow with the auction house in Sweet Willow. He doesn't sound too promising. He only wants a woman to help him with the band of boys he's taken in."

Harriet snorted. "A marriage of convenience. How romantic. I wonder if he expects you to fetch his slippers."

"I wouldn't mind fetching slippers if I could find Abigail. Wouldn't it be something if he knew my sister. How big is Sweet Willow, I wonder?"

"I don't know. But an auction house is certainly more promising than the butcher." Harriet turned the envelope in her hand before taking out the letter. "Think of his auction wares! Gems and fine art and furnishings! I like this one already. Let's see if Mr. Convenience mentions his slippers."

Sarah waited for Harriet to read the letter as she watched the flames in the hearth. The flickering fire mesmerized her. Thoughts of the sister she might never meet faded from her mind. She held her hand to the warmth, as she considered writing Mr. and Mrs. Caldicott and asking for money so she could return home to San Francisco.

"Heavens," Harriet said softly.

Sarah turned. Harriet held her hand to her heart. She was flushed, her eyes wide with shock as she stared at the letter. Sarah hurried to her side, wondering what on earth had come over Harriet.

"What is it?" Sarah asked. "What's upset you so?"

Harriet went to a desk in the corner of the parlor and returned with a ledger. Sarah watched, a mix of curiosity and alarm. Sarah knew very little of pregnancy, but felt certain that in her condition, Harriet shouldn't allow herself such strong emotions.

After she sat on the chesterfield, she opened the ledger.

"This is a list of the accounts Abigail used to keep for my family. She was so good. So careful."

Sarah held her breath as she lowered to sit beside Harriet. She studied her sister's writing, fascinated by the penmanship, yet unsure why Harriet felt the need to show her.

"You see how she liked to add a tiny heart, here and there?" Harriet ran her finger under an entry. "It was a heart within a heart. Two hearts, really."

Sarah nodded. "I see."

"Your sister did so much for our family. I never realized how much until later. She even helped me write letters to Mr. Walker." Harriet held the letter from the man in Sweet Willow. With a trembling hand, she set it next to the entries in the ledger. She traced the last line, stopping at the heart that adorned the final words. A heart within a heart.

"Your sister wrote this man's letter," Harriet whispered. "I'm sure of it."

Chapter Ten

Holden

Holden kicked the clod of dirt. It sailed through the air and landed with a thump. He was so mad that he could spit and might have if spitting would make him feel better. The fancy lady at church had talked about Noah needing a helpmeet. That had been four days ago, but Holden was still steamed.

She'd given them a sappy look like they were just a bunch of snot-nosed kids. He kicked another clod of dirt. He was on his way to the barn to mend a bridle and he was grateful for some time to think. At times, a man couldn't mull things over unless he was alone.

Snow White! Did that lady think she was being funny? Did she think they were just a bunch of babies?

If there was one thing Holden disliked more than anything in the world, it was to be treated like a child. At twelve, he considered himself already grown. A man. Even Noah seemed to think he was a grown-up. Noah considered Holden responsible enough to take care of important matters.

Take the line-up at the auction barn, for example. When Holden first began work in the barn, the task of getting the animals into the pen in the right order had fallen to an older fellow. Johnny. The old-timer had to leave Sweet Willow for a few weeks, heading out on a cattle drive. Noah gave the job to Holden and the boy had worked the line-up ever since.

At the end of every sale day, Noah praised Holden for how well he managed.

Which only proved that Holden was a grown man.

Noah also entrusted Holden with keeping order amongst the boys. Noah hadn't ever said that exactly, but Holden knew that's how he felt, and nothing was more important than Noah's respect. The boy felt it keenly.

Noah was the finest man Holden had ever known. Which was the very reason he had no wish for a mama. None. And despite all the quarreling amongst the boys, he knew they'd agree. Maybe not Josiah, but he was the baby and therefore didn't matter.

The time had come, he decided. After he finished mending the bridle, he called a meeting amongst the boys. It took some time to track them down but eventually they gathered in the feed room. The grain sacks and overturned buckets offered a place to sit so they could come up with a plan. Holden waited until the last boy settled and closed the door.

"I thought Noah was just kidding around," Holden said solemnly. "But I'm starting to worry that he's serious."

"About what?" Josiah scratched his head, frowning.

"About marrying some lady!" Holden exclaimed.

"Like you weren't the one who wrote her a letter," Dustin grumbled, frowning at Josiah. "After we told you not to."

Josiah's brows lifted. "I wrote one but Noah said he'd already sent one. He said he'd send it later on, when the lady wrote back."

Holden crossed his arms the same way Noah did when he wanted to explain things. "Know what's going to happen if he gets married, don't you?"

No one replied.

Holden paced the length of the feed room, turned and walked back. It always helped to wait a spell before going on. Noah did that. Pastor James did that too every Sunday. Pacing was what men did to make sure folks were paying attention.

"I'll tell you what's going to happen," Holden said solemnly. "Babies. That's what."

Josiah yelped. "She's bringing babies?"

The boys gave a collective groan. Walt reached over and swatted the top of Josiah's head. A few snickered at Josiah's scowl and threatening gestures.

"No, dummy." Holden shook his head. "That's what happens when a man and lady get married. They start having babies right away."

"Not right after," Dustin countered. "It takes four and a half months."

Walt scoffed at this. "That's not true. It takes ten days, I think. Or a hundred days. I forget how many zeros but not four and a half months."

The boys all offered varying opinions on the Walt and Dustin claims. Some thought it had nothing to do with time but with seasons of the year, just like spring lambs. This notion elicited gales of laughter. They joked about spring babies until Hugo assured them babies came at Christmas. Everyone knew that Christmas was the time for little babies.

Adding to the confusion was the fact that not one boy knew his own birthday. Walt insisted his was February thirty-first, but no one believed him. Harold argued that Walt was fibbing, talking about his birthday while the rest of them didn't have one to speak of. "He's just putting on airs."

"Hush, all of y'all," Holden demanded. "It doesn't matter. What matters is that if Noah has his own kin, where do you think that leaves us?"

Quiet filled the room.

Holden resisted the urge to keep talking. He let the silence sit there for a moment to let the boys stew a little. It wasn't until both Josiah and Hugo sniffled that Holden went on. "He promised he wouldn't get rid of us, but that was before he started talking about getting married. I'm telling y'all this changes everything. If he gets a wife, we'll need to work together."

The boys nodded.

"We'll figure out a plan to make sure she doesn't stick around too long. Clear?"

Each of the boys agreed. Together they could thwart Noah's plans for taking a wife. And if they could manage that, they wouldn't have to worry about any pesky babies no matter when they got born.

Chapter Eleven

Sarah

The next few days were scarcely more than a blur. At first, Harriet seemed very pleased that she'd discovered the letter was from Abigail's hand. Soon after, she grew fretful at the prospect of Sarah leaving Boston, however. She made outlandish offers, trying to tempt Sarah to stay with her.

Sarah was touched by Harriet's invitation to remain with her in her home. She could not, however, give up her quest to find Abigail. After she made the necessary arrangements with Mr. Perryman, the portly gentleman at the matchmaker's office, she counted the days until her ship, *The Sparrow,* would leave.

Harriet fussed about the travel arrangements. She insisted on paying for a first-class cabin for Sarah. Once that was done, she took Sarah shopping.

"Your dresses are very pretty," she said as they walked along some of Boston's finest shops. "But you'll need more than muslin and broadcloth. And a few extra pairs of boots. And sleeping gowns."

The list went on. After all was said and done, Sarah needed two extra trunks. Harriet was more than happy to embark on another shopping trip.

Harriet put on a brave and cheerful face the day *The Sparrow* set sail. "You'll write me, won't you? And tell Abigail how sorry I am?"

"I will write you as soon as I arrive."

"And tell me about your auctioneer," she said. "And about his, er, rather large brood."

Sarah smiled. "I hope he doesn't expect me to bring his slippers."

"And I hope he lets you have first dibs on the gems and paintings."

They said a tearful goodbye. Sarah boarded the ship and stood on the railing, waving to the crowd. She remained on the deck, and watched the harbor fade in the distance, hardly able to believe she was on yet another journey.

Traveling on a sailing ship proved equal parts exhilarating and lonesome. The first few nights, she took dinner in her room. Her cabin, Number 16 in first class, was spacious, luxurious even, but the long evenings alone left her feeling fretful about her plan. She tried to distract herself with one of the many books she'd packed.

Nothing held her attention.

She thought about Otto's books back in San Francisco, dozens of volumes about cowboy adventure and tales of the Wild West. If only she had such a book to read. It would be a comfort to read about cowboys and their world. Oh, she knew it was made up and likely not true. And yet, the stories would serve to remind her of Otto as well as transport her to the rugged land of the cowboy.

Once again, she'd set out on a journey to find Abigail, only this time she wasn't traveling to Boston to search for her. She traveled to Texas, but it might as well have been China from the stories she'd heard. The only reason to go was Abigail. And

Abigail, if she was still in Texas, would not be waiting for her at the dock. A man would be there. With six children. Her very own cowboy. Noah Bailey.

She could hardly imagine what sort of man he might be. He would be a kind man, she assured herself. After all, he'd taken in all those poor children. She liked to think of Noah as a soft-spoken, gentle man, but at times fearful thoughts came to her. Particularly in the dead of night.

He wanted a marriage of convenience. What if he changed the terms? What then? He might be a hard, brutal man who treated women like they were his possessions. She'd heard of such men.

As the ship plowed the waters of the Atlantic, Sarah's dread grew. How had she allowed herself to consider this foolhardy venture? She fretted over that very question, at times blaming herself, other times blaming Mrs. Penobscot. It wasn't Mrs. Penobscot's fault, of course, but in her darkest moments, she was willing to cast blame on everyone who came to mind.

Mr. Perryman had presented her with a book on home management. She recalled the book a few days into the journey and forced herself to read a little each day. She read tips on cooking and keeping a home. Somehow, she didn't think she needed to learn about managing staff. Mr. Bailey had some means, but she assumed no butler. Or under-butler. She smiled at the thought. Mrs. Penobscot would approve if she did, in fact, have a butler and under-butler.

Noah Bailey probably didn't have a staff. He did have a house full of growing boys, however. She paid careful attention to the references to easy cookery for the new bride. The recipes seemed simple enough. Her confidence grew as she recalled some of the savory dishes Erna made. She imagined serving her hungry brood buttery noodles and schnitzel. They'd gaze at her adoringly as she offered them seconds.

As time went on, she would learn their favorites and perhaps even bake some of Erna's special Austrian apple cake or plum turnovers. If the way to a man's heart was through his stomach, she'd have to make certain to cook well enough for the hearts of a houseful of men.

On the fifth night, after evenings confined to her room, she resolved to dine in the first-class dining room. She required company. That was what ailed her. The solitude of the cabin had become too much for her to bear. She sorted through her dresses and selected a pale blue silk with ruched sleeves and a lace collar.

Before she left her room, she studied herself in the mirror. Otto and Erna, if they could see her, would complement her blue eyes and how well the blue dress suited her. Otto teased that her angelic eyes made up for her wicked disarray of curls. Erna always shushed him for she loved Sarah's curls.

Sarah always bound her hair into a neat bun when she worked in the Beckers' candy shop. On Sundays as well. But in the evenings at suppertime, she would wear it down. If pressed, she would have to admit some vanity about the thick curls that trailed past her shoulders. She considered her hair to be her best feature.

The sad memories of Otto and Erna faded from her mind as she touched one of her flaxen locks. What would Noah Bailey think of her hair? Or her eyes? Her heart beat a little faster as she imagined him looking upon her with approval. Perhaps she might convince him to forgive her for coming to Texas under false pretenses.

She pushed the thoughts aside, left her cabin and went to the dining room. As she made her way, a new round of worry assailed her. She knew no one on the ship. Perhaps she'd have to sit by herself, a notion which sent a shiver of humiliation across her.

After a wrong turn, she found herself in an unfamiliar part of the ship. She tried to retrace her steps to no avail. The long hallways led through the first-class cabins but did not lead to Number 16.

"This is ridiculous," she muttered, stopping to study the number of a corner cabin. "How did I manage to get lost on a ship?"

She wandered down to the end and stopped, looking back and forth as she tried to decide which direction to choose. The hallways were empty.

A cabin door opened. A man stepped out of his room and regarded her with curiosity.

"Why aren't you a pretty lil thing."

Sarah wanted to ask the man for directions but thought better of it. His hair stuck up at odd angles. His eyes were bloodshot. He was dressed in fine clothes, yet his shirt and pants were rumpled. He wore only one shoe.

Clearly, he was inebriated. It smelled as if he'd bathed in whiskey. If she was going to ask for help, she'd need to find someone who knew his way and hadn't overindulged in spirits.

She hurried away.

"Hey there, girlie. I'm talking to you." With a quick backwards glance, she found him shuffling after her. A yelp broke the silence of the hallway. To her embarrassment, she realized the humiliating sound had come from her own lips.

Reaching the end of the hall, she discovered, with horror, that she'd arrived at a dead end. She whirled around to face her pursuer.

"Stay away from me." She held up her pocketbook, as if that might offer hope of protection.

"You got the prettiest eyes I've ever seen."

In truth, her eyes were a source of pride to her. She usually tried not to take delight in compliments about her eyes. Pride was, after all, a sin.

The man stepped closer, looming over her. His lips pulled back into a hideous sneer. She'd never been so near a stranger. She shrank against the wall and let out a strangled cry.

A door opened some distance away. Sarah tried to call for help. She parted her lips, trying desperately to beg the woman to come to her aid, but the words stuck in her throat.

A woman spoke. "Oh, dear. How very ghastly."

"Not again," came another feminine voice. "Tsk, tsk."

Sarah managed to say a single word. "No," she whispered.

"Yes," the man replied. He swayed and belched. A putrid stench filled the air between them. Sarah whimpered. It was all like a terrible dream, the sort of dream where no matter what, she couldn't save herself from a terrifying ordeal.

Suddenly, the man jerked his shoulders back. "Ow!" He howled. "Dadgum it! Let me be."

Sarah's jaw dropped as the man lurched away. His arms windmilled as he danced around the hallway. Hopping from one foot to the other, he crashed into a wall. He let out another screeching cry, arched his back and staggered to the other side where he landed with a breathtaking thud.

She wasn't sure if she was dreaming or if this astonishing spectacle was truly taking place. Never had she witnessed anything like this man's antics. Perhaps he was mad.

Two women stood a few steps from the stricken man. Neither woman seemed at all perplexed by what had just happened. They remained still, unmoving, with their hands clasped as they studied the man with vague interest. When he saw them, he bellowed and held up his hands as if to ward them off. "Please. No."

"My sister and I have decided we don't like you," one of the women said, her tone bland. "Do we, Gertie?"

"Not in the least, Bess," the other lady replied. "But we don't *despise* you, just yet. That response is coming. Let me assure you, and when my sister despises someone, she tends to be unkind. Very unkind. Some might even say cruel."

The two women laughed.

"Hush, Gertie. Speak for yourself."

The first woman went on. "My sister is not a terribly nice person under the best of circumstances."

Gertie sighed and adjusted the sleeve of her gown. "So unfair. Really."

Sarah watched in disbelief. The two women were older, perhaps in their fifties, and slight. They hardly seemed as though they could frighten a mouse, and yet, the drunken passenger regarded them with dread.

The first one, Gertie, went on in a bored tone as if commenting on last week's weather. "The last time Bess confronted a man she despised, he spent a considerable amount of time in the hospital."

Bess shook her head and gave her sister an indignant look. "Define considerable."

Gertie ignored her and continued to address the man. "From the hospital he moved into a lovely pine box, about 18 inches tall."

"Pure slander."

"Do you want to know the best thing about traveling on a ship?"

The man by now had crawled to the wall and sat with his back against it. He blinked. Tears fell from his eyes. He snuffled. "N-n-no."

Both women regarded him with disappointment, their brows lifted. Gertie tilted her head a notch. "Are you *sure* you don't want to know?"

"Y-yes," the man stammered. He gulped. "Actually, I do. Very much. Please tell me."

The sisters smiled. This time Gertie spoke. "The best thing about traveling on a ship is the notion of burial at sea."

The man paled.

The ladies both laughed uproariously. They were so overcome, both had to wipe tears from their eyes. It took a moment, maybe two, for the two ladies to recover from the hilarity. Bess gave her sister an appreciative look as if complimenting her on her wit.

Sarah remained still, too shocked to move. She considered the small but formidable women. They were like a pair of gray-haired avenging angels. They wore solemn dresses, immaculate but from a forgotten decade of fashion. Their hair was swept into tidy arrangements. Despite their treatment of the drunken passenger, they looked every inch the respectable, first-class passengers.

Sarah wondered if they were in fact joking about burials at sea. The man clearly didn't think they jested. He blubbered, took out a handkerchief and wiped his brow, snuffling and muttering.

Gertie stepped closer, her smile fading. "If I see you trying to force your affections on a hapless young woman, Mr. Richards, I will make certain you face justice."

"Lord have mercy. You know my name?" he asked.

"I do, in fact. I learned your name moments after you made the chambermaid cry. She came to our cabin after you chased her around yours, insisting she kiss you."

Mr. Richards opened his mouth and stared helplessly.

"My name is Gertie, and this is my sister, Bess. Our last name is Payne." She arched a brow, as if her point needed emphasis. It did not. Mr. Richards looked as if he might faint straight away.

"Payne?" he whimpered.

"Indeed." She continued. "Now, go to your room. Throw away every drop of whiskey. Get yourself to bed so you can sleep off your state of intoxication. And when you wake in the morning, *if* you're sober, say your prayers, confess your ghastly transgressions and ask forgiveness."

"Forgiveness?" he murmured.

"That's what I said. You will ask forgiveness from your *maker*."

"Maker..." he echoed.

"Best do that *before* you meet Him," added Gertie's sister with a wink. "I'd imagine you don't want to ask forgiveness from the inside of a pine box."

The man began to weep. His panicked gaze went back and forth between the two ladies. He struggled to his feet, and with a whimper, he sprinted down the hallway with surprising alacrity, entered his room and slammed the door behind him.

Chapter Twelve

Noah

Noah slated the first Saturday of the month for the sale of horses. The prior owner of the Sweet Willow Auction House always offered a broad choice of livestock on sale day. He'd thrown all the critters out there without any care at all. Noah determined early on it was better to sell sheep and goats on a different day than cattle. Having all manner of animals in the stock barns led to pandemonium.

Noah's niece, Francine, liked to come to the horse sales and took a spot overlooking the sale pen so she could have a bird's-eye view. There had been a time when she was his little shadow, but since he'd taken in the boys, she'd decided she didn't want to traipse around after him anymore. She made no secret of the fact that the boys annoyed her.

She sat at his desk, looking over the auction docket. "Half the horses are draft horses."

"They arrived last night from Humber Falls. Fine-looking animals."

Noah stood beside the desk, surveying the goings-on below. Holden and his two brothers raked the pen. They chatted about something or other, taking their sweet time. At least they worked steadily while Josiah stood by the wheelbarrow staring off into the wild blue yonder. Typical.

"Josiah," Noah called.

Not one of the boys looked up. Holden and his two brothers had busted out laughing from Harold's antics. Josiah remained by the wheelbarrow, unmoving, oblivious to his surroundings.

Noah cupped his hands to his mouth. "*JoSIah!*"

The boy's shoulders jerked. He glanced around the pen, searching for the person who had called his name. Noah waved his hands over his head.

Josiah grinned. "Yessir?"

"Quit your woolgathering."

The boy's mouth opened, hanging wide for a moment before he snapped it shut. He pressed his lips to form a small line of protest. He didn't argue, however.

Noah's crew of boys might be a pain in the neck at times, but not one of them argued with him. They had respect. They had manners. For that he was grateful.

Francine shook her head and gave him a pitying look. She seemed to think his life was now pure misery.

Noah suppressed a smile.

He was about to brag on one of them, but he thought better of it. Francine would not want to hear anything positive about his boys. But he wanted to tell her. That morning, Walt had produced his finest batch of biscuits so far. Hardly burned at all. A rumor had circulated the breakfast table. Some of the boys suggested Walt had dropped half the biscuits on the floor while putting them in the breadbasket. Noah had refrained from asking for details.

The stands in the auction barn were beginning to fill with ranchers and townsfolk. Noah spied his brother, Seth, looking for a seat. Noah went downstairs to say hello.

"Stopped by the post office," Seth said, envelope in hand. "It's from Boston."

"Thank you," Noah said, as he took the letter, his tone even.

His heart leapt inside his chest. He didn't want to appear too eager, though. Seth would just give him a bad time about seeking out a mail-order bride. Turnaround was fair play, Noah had to admit. He tucked the letter into his shirt pocket.

Seth shook his head, grinning. "I know you're dying to open it."

"I'll get to it, by and by."

"How was breakfast this morning?"

"Why do you ask?"

"Can't I ask a simple question?"

"You never ask about breakfast. Why now?"

"I chatted with Holden. He told me Walt's taken over breakfast duty."

"That's right," Noah said cautiously.

"Holden said he dumped the entire pan of biscuits on the floor."

Noah frowned. "Holden better watch his step. He might get breakfast assigned to him. He'll have to wake up a half hour early and listen to everyone gripe."

Seth nodded and wandered off to find a spot in the stands.

Over the next hour, Noah tried to find a quiet moment to read the letter. To no avail. There were a hundred details that required his attention, and before long, it was time to start the auction. The stands were crowded with buyers and sellers. They didn't like to be kept waiting and Noah prided himself on being prompt. As the clock struck ten o'clock, he started the bidding on the first horse.

The day passed quickly with higher sales than Noah expected. The final tally of figures told Noah he'd set a record for the first Saturday horse sales.

Later, after supper, Noah sat on the back porch to read his letter. Finally.

All day he'd imagined reading a letter from a young woman who wanted to begin corresponding with him. It would be the first of many letters, he figured, and along the way, Noah would know, somehow, if she might be a good match. He wanted to be married soon. Very soon. But he couldn't hurry things along. That was how a man ended up with the wrong woman.

When he opened the envelope, he didn't find a letter written with a feminine hand. Instead, the letter had been written by Mr. Perryman, the owner of Massachusetts Matchmaking Company. His heart sank to his boots. Noah read the man's words to find that a bride had been selected and was on her way.

Noah growled, crumpled the letter and paced the back porch.

This was not what he'd expected. Not even close. He needed to get to know a woman before agreeing to marry. What if the lady who stepped off the boat was some sort of bad-tempered woman who despised children? What if she arrived with six of her own children in tow? What if...?

Noah's imagination took off like a horse bolting from the barn on a spring day.

When, he wondered, would the woman he did *not* pick arrive in Galveston? He straightened the crumpled letter and read it once more. At the bottom, written as if an afterthought, Mr. Perryman had added a note. The unwanted bride would arrive in Galveston. In three days.

Chapter Thirteen

Sarah

After the incident in the hallway, the ship's captain began sending an officer to escort Sarah to the first-class dining room. At first, she wanted to refuse. She was embarrassed. The officers, however, were charming and cordial, and she relented. Each time it was a different young man, a dashing fellow who told her tales of far-off lands as he walked her to the dining room.

Once there, she was seated with her new friends, Bess and Gertie Payne. The captain stopped by the table most evenings to say hello. He assured the ladies that Mr. Richards would be dealt with if he troubled them or any other female passengers.

Bess and Gertie were moving to Texas to escape the cold northeast. They had their summer free and intended to visit Bolivar Island to indulge in bird watching. The women were lovely dinner companions. Sarah couldn't bring herself to reveal her reasons for traveling to Texas. Since the first evening together, she'd told them she was visiting her sister.

As the days passed, the entire venture troubled her more. On the last evening, she could hardly eat a bite of her meal. Worry gnawed inside her.

"What's troubling you, dear?" Bess asked, gently.

"Why don't you tell us the real reason you're traveling to Texas?" her sister added, a smile curving her lips. "Bess and I have been schoolteachers for over twenty years. We know when someone's hiding something."

A few days before, Sarah might have considered trying to plead innocent. Not tonight. It was her last night on the ship. Tomorrow, she'd meet the man she'd promised to marry. Tears stung her eyes, earning her a startled look from the two sisters.

"Oh, dear, please don't cry. It can't be all that bad, can it?" Bess asked. "Shall we steal you away to Bolivar Island?"

Sarah shook her head and dabbed the linen napkin at the corner of each eye. "I do intend to meet my sister, if I can find her. First, I'll marry, however. A Texan gentleman sent for a mail-order wife." She smiled tearfully. "And I accepted his offer."

The two sisters looked back and forth at each other and to her. Both wore looks of surprise, but not expressions of complete shock. For that, Sarah was grateful.

"That's lovely," Gertie murmured.

"He's taken in six motherless children and is trying to raise them on his own."

"Oh, my," Gertie exclaimed. "I would be crying too."

"He sounds like a very noble man." Bess took a sip of her tea. "And he's lucky to have you."

Gertie agreed. The ladies began to ask a hundred questions about Noah, his boys, his home. Sarah wished she could have answered their questions more fully, but the truth was, she knew very little.

In the days before she traveled to Boston, and again before the ship left, Sarah had imagined meeting Abigail. It would be a sunny day. Sarah would serve tea and a special cake, perhaps Erna's Lemon Delight, or maybe a berry tart.

78

Whatever she served would be perfect for a talk between sisters.

Sarah would wear the pale blue dress, the one she'd bought for that very occasion. Abigail might wear a similar color, especially if the two girls favored each other. Sarah's imaginings filled her with happiness.

Or they did when she thought of Abigail.

That night, she lay in bed and gazed out the window at the night sky. Tomorrow, she'd meet Noah. And tomorrow, she'd confess the thing that had troubled her since leaving Boston; part of the reason she'd come to Texas was to find her sister. She closed her eyes and prayed that Noah Bailey wouldn't consider her a liar, or a cheat. Or worse.

Chapter Fourteen

Noah

Folks at Galveston Pier showed up in their finest duds, Noah observed as he strolled the wooden pier. The wind ruffled the calm water. The blue, blue sky held not even a speck of a cloud. The crowd grew with each passing moment, gathering along the waterfront, smiling, laughing. A sense of excitement grew, especially when a mast appeared way, way in the distance.

It was still too early to tell if it was *The Sparrow*.

He congratulated himself on getting his boys up an hour before dawn, washed, dressed and all the way to Galveston with time to spare. He'd considered getting a hotel in Galveston but figured that would be pressing his luck.

While the boys were a sight better than they were when he first took them in several months ago, they were still an unruly bunch, given to arguments, jostling and the occasional cussing. Throw in a little fighting and it was clear his family wasn't ready for Galveston's Driscoll Hotel. That was where his brother stayed when he came to fetch Laura. No, it would be some time before he was ready to brave a fancy outfit like the Driscoll.

Although, he had to admit the boys were doing fine, or at least they were doing fine right now. The six of them sat on a bench, side by side, enjoying ice cream cones. None of them were inclined to squabble when they had an ice cream in hand.

Holden, the eldest, finished first and came to his side. The boy had been sullen ever since Noah told him about the trip to Galveston. The ice cream had helped matters considerably. That, and that Noah had a talk with him about Sarah. It always helped to talk to Holden man-to-man.

"There's a boat out there," Holden said.

"I see that."

Noah suppressed a smile. Holden and his two brothers were usually quiet and thoughtful. When they spoke, they often pointed out something that was clearly evident.

"You think it's *The Sparrow*?"

Noah glanced at his watch. "Probably. They're not expecting another ship until tomorrow."

At the far end of the pier, a group burst into song. A man played a fiddle. People clapped and sang.

"Some folks singing down there," Holden said.

"You don't say."

Holden's mouth tipped with a rare smile. Noah recalled the first time he set eyes on the boys. They huddled in a cold, misting rain on the train depot in Sweet Willow. Holden kept a watchful eye on all of them, his expression hollow and defeated. Noah would never forget the look in the boy's eyes.

The wariness and silence lasted some time. They'd accepted his help. Offered a polite word of thanks here and there. But for the most part, all the boys watched him with suspicion. It was as if they expected the worst of him. They couldn't allow themselves to believe he really only wanted to lend a hand.

Over time, they settled in and began acting like boys. Joking. Fighting. Being a nuisance and pain in his neck. But it was Holden who was the last to trust him. The last to smile.

He was pensive. The boy might point out the obvious, but he might just as easily say something thoughtful and helpful. He was probably quiet because he was so busy growing. In the last three months, he'd grown a head taller. Noah had bought him new pants twice. It seemed the moment the boy put them on, they were three inches too short.

"Germans."

Holden's comment startled Noah from his thoughts. "What now?"

"The people singing and playing a tune. They're German. Probably from Fredericksburg or maybe New Braunfels."

Noah listened for a moment. He didn't recognize the song and couldn't make out the words. A couple began to dance on the pier. They were older, gray-haired but danced with remarkable grace and pep. The crowd clapped, keeping time with the music.

"They got good peaches in Fredericksburg," Holden remarked. "Me and my brothers worked in the orchards for a month last year."

"I like peaches," Noah said, turning his attention back to the approaching ship. Sometimes he thought he sounded like he was pointing out the obvious, just like Holden and his brothers. The trouble was, he never liked to ask the boys too many questions about their past. All of them had lived through hard times. Noah never wanted to stir up bad memories.

He'd imagined the boys would be happy when he told them he intended to take a wife. He thought the notion of a womanly influence in their raucous, messy home would please them. It seemed, though, that only Josiah was happy about things.

Holden told Noah that morning he didn't want a woman's influence, thank you very much. He'd been let down too many times by a woman. Starting with his own mother.

All the boys had been let down or, put in harsher terms, abandoned. All of them missed out on a father and yearned for a father-figure, but it was a mother they missed the most. In the deep of night, when one called out from a bad dream, they didn't call for a father.

Noah kept his gaze fixed on the advancing ship. The prow cut the waves, sending a spray arching over the water. As the ship neared, the spray caught the sunshine. Droplets glimmered with rainbow colors. The boys, finished with their ice creams, shouted and pointed with excitement as *The Sparrow* approached the pier.

Distantly, he noted the music. The laughter. The boys' growing excitement. He gave thanks for the ship's safe arrival. He added a prayer that God would bless his family with a gentle, good-hearted woman.

The sailors aboard the ship yelled a greeting to the crew on the pier. They exchanged insults as they tossed ropes over the railing. A good-natured, if not entirely wholesome, banter followed as the men worked to secure the vessel.

Noah held his breath, scanning the passengers. Sarah was up there somewhere. The notion seemed hard to believe. The crowd aboard the boat was lively. Young and old. A few children. None that seemed like they might be his Sarah, or not from where he stood.

The boys gathered around him. They jabbered. They joked and busted out laughing at each other's pranks. Noah hardly heard.

When the gangway was in place, the first passenger disembarked. She was stout, red-faced with four children trailing behind her.

"Why, there she is now," Holden exclaimed.

Noah turned to stare at the boy. "What?"

Holden ignored him, cupped his hand to his mouth and yelled. "Hello, Miss Sarah!"

The boys craned their necks, lifting to their tiptoes, trying to see over the crowd. Noah frowned. How could Holden know which of the ladies was Sarah?

"We're over here, Mother!"

"You see her?" Noah asked, bewildered by Holden's certainty that he had spotted Sarah.

Holden pointed at the woman on the gangway. "I believe that's her."

The woman peered through the crowd. She was short and rather plump. When Holden yelled another cheerful greeting, she scowled and drew back with clear dismay. With an indignant jerk of her chin, she marched off to the throng of Germans, her brood following.

"Guess not," Holden muttered. He shrugged and then grinned at Noah. Sparks of amusement fairly danced in the boy's eyes.

For a moment, Noah forgot about the ship and the passengers and the girl from Boston. That morning, he'd alluded to his concerns about what kind of woman would step off the ship. Would she be an older lady? Perhaps with children of her own? Holden must have decided Noah's concerns were fair game and formed a plan to tease him.

Noah tousled the boy's hair and grumbled under his breath. "You little stinker."

Holden's chuckle grew to a deep belly laugh.

Usually, the boys kept their ribbing to each other. Every so often one would direct some gentle teasing at him. Almost every time, they'd catch him unawares which only added to their delight.

"Mr. Bailey," a man's voice called. "Mr. Noah Bailey."

A man in uniform stood at the top of the gangway. He was older, with graying hair and shoulders erect with unmistakable authority. In an instant, Noah knew it was the captain of *The Sparrow*.

His heart tumbled to his feet. What if something had happened to Sarah? While he'd worried about her being older, or with a child on each hip, he hadn't worried overly much if she was safe.

He pushed his way through the crowd. When he reached the bottom of the gangway, he waved to the man. He wanted to call out but could not. The words refused to leave his mouth. His throat tightened as if stuck in a steel vise.

"Hey, over here," shouted Holden.

The captain nodded and descended the gangway.

"I'm Captain Markwell," he said, offering his hand to Noah. "Your intended, Miss Sarah Becker, is under my care after a small mishap on board a few days into the journey. She's fine. Just a little flustered. I made certain to provide an escort to her so she wouldn't need to walk the halls of the ship unattended."

"Mighty kind of you, Captain." Noah's thoughts churned. "I'm obliged."

"It was no trouble," the captain said with a chuckle. "Sarah is delightful. My officers thought her quite agreeable. Not one complained about escorting her to the first-class dining room. I think they all vied for a chance."

The captain's words turned Noah's thoughts abruptly from worry to irritation. Sarah escorted by sailors? His attention moved to the top of the gangway where a young lady stood, shaking the hand of one of the officers of *The Sparrow*.

"There she is now," the captain said.

Noah felt the air leave his lungs. He stared, hardly daring to breathe. She was fair, middling height with hair the color of honey. The deep blue of her dress made her skin look soft. A ridiculous notion took over his thoughts. He wondered if her skin would feel soft. A rush of heat warmed his face. He shoved the thought aside.

Sarah didn't realize she was being watched. She brushed a lock of blonde hair from her eyes, smiled at something one of the men said. She seemed reticent and held herself back, which eased his irritation somewhat, but then she replied with a remark that the officers seemed to find amusing. All of them laughed heartily.

"I should introduce you," the captain said, his tone jovial.

"Sure hate to interrupt her little visit," Noah growled.

The boys milled around him, clamoring to know if the lady in the blue dress was indeed Sarah.

The captain called out. The sound drew Sarah's attention. She looked at the captain before shifting her gaze to Noah. Her lips parted with surprise. When the captain beckoned her, she began her descent. One of the officers offered his arm but she refused with a slight shake of her head.

"That girl can't be much older than me," Holden exclaimed.

"She's eighteen," the captain said.

Noah kept his gaze fixed on Sarah but battled his irritation once more. He wasn't sure what it was that got under his skin. Maybe it was all the men in dapper uniforms. Maybe it was the fact that the captain knew her age. Either way, he felt a tad hot under the collar. Noah had to admit, if only to himself, that he didn't know much of anything about his intended. He wondered if the uniformed fellas watching her descend the gangway knew she was eighteen.

He had the urge to storm up the gangway and give a few of them a good shove or better. Not the best example for the boys, but there it was.

"Eighteen! Why, she's only six years older 'an me!" Holden replied with a huff.

The captain went on. "Sarah's birthday is in September. Soon she'll be *nineteen*."

Noah gritted his teeth.

The officers drew together and burst into song with perfect harmony. A melody about Sweet Sarah. They sang farewell to the girl with eyes of summer's morn and a bunch of other nonsense. Their voices floated across the harbor as Sarah slowly and carefully descended the gangway. They finished with a chorus about her returning soon.

The crowd clapped. Sarah colored.

"You got to be kidding me," Noah growled.

"That sounded nice," said Josiah. "I wonder if they know-"

"Hush, Josiah," Noah snapped.

When Sarah reached the end of the gangway, she stopped and offered him a shy smile. A blush bloomed across her cheeks as she looked at him with the prettiest eyes he'd ever seen. She held out a trembling hand. "Hello, Mr. Bailey. I'm very pleased to meet you."

Chapter Fifteen

Sarah

Mr. Bailey insisted she call him Noah. After all, they were about to say their vows. She knew that, of course, but that didn't mean it was easy to call him by his given name. She found herself inclined to address the gruff man as Mr. Bailey.

Harriet's words rang in her mind. *Let's see if Mr. Convenience expects you to fetch his slippers...*

Mr. Convenience didn't look like a man who fancied slippers. He was nicely dressed, to be sure. With a crisp white shirt, open at the collar, a vest, dark trousers and boots, he looked every inch the Texan. No slippers for Mr. Bailey.

He was a head taller than her. From the single letter she'd read, she knew he was twenty-five, only seven years her senior, but with his take-charge manner, he seemed much older. Without asking, Sarah also knew Noah's auction house didn't trade in gems or fine paintings. Harriet would be disappointed. He had to know Abigail, however. That was all Sarah cared about.

Now it was just a matter of summoning the courage to ask.

While he and the boys loaded her trunks onto the back of the wagon, he spoke in a brusque, clipped tone. Twice.

His words had been directed at the boys, but it still made her respond with a wave of alarm. Both times, she'd retreated a step or two.

The boys didn't seem overly worried, however. She watched with interest as the group worked together to lift and position the trunks. She wasn't entirely sure where she should stand while she waited. Wagons rumbled past. Men on horseback, dressed in cowboy attire, trotted by, tipping their hats as they passed.

"Think you brought enough?" Noah asked as they set the last trunk in place.

She blinked, not sure how to respond to his grumpy tone. Noah Bailey was unlike any other man she'd known. He was a far cry from dear, sweet Otto who never fussed or raised his voice.

"Did I bring enough?" she asked timidly.

"Joking," he replied. He added a wink, but his mouth remained fixed in a grim line.

If that was his expression when he was joking, she hated to think what he looked like when he was angry. The boys clambered to the back of the wagon and watched the surrounding activity with interest.

"I think we ought to say our vows here in Galveston," Noah said, coming to her side.

She wasn't sure if that was a statement or a proposal. Biting her lip, she tried to think of what to say. A hundred times or more, she'd imagined this moment, but somehow it had always seemed different. Less dust in the air. Fewer crowds and clatter. Perhaps even a little moonlight.

He waited for a reply.

"Vows here in Galveston. Er. Yes. Right."

He knit his brow, probably wondering if she was daft. It was the right thing to do, of course. She'd come to marry the man after all, and she couldn't live under the same roof if they were unmarried. Even if it was just a marriage of convenience.

"Do you have a church in mind?"

"No church. A judge."

Her heart sank. Their marriage was an arrangement, nothing more. She shouldn't press for anything like exchanging vows with a man of the cloth. Noah Bailey was clearly a practical man.

"All right." She schooled her features, hoping she appeared cheerful. "That would be fine."

"Let me help you up."

Taking her elbow, he ushered her to the wagon. His touch was gentle but firm and sent a tingle up her arm. The sensation wasn't wholly unpleasant, she decided. She stole a glance at his profile, wishing she could ask him about Abigail. How had it come to pass that her sister had helped this man write a letter?

Before she could say a word, she felt his hands move to her waist. One moment she stood beside him, the next she found herself aloft and seated on the wagon bench.

She looked for Bess and Gertie, hoping that from the vantage point of the wagon, she might spy the two sisters. The dock of Galveston was too crowded, too noisy.

In her haste, Sarah hadn't even said goodbye. The ladies were on their way to see birds on nearby Bolivar Island. After spending each evening with them in the dining room, she'd grown fond of the wise and witty older ladies. The notion she might not see them again felt heavy on her heart.

It was absurd, really. But Sarah cared for the ladies and enjoyed their friendship. After they plucked her from certain peril, she'd sought them out every chance. She enjoyed their company, even if they did seem overly fond of the subject of birds. They'd spent most afternoons strolling the decks, field glasses in hand while Bess and Gertie waxed poetic about killdeer, coots and cormorants.

She wished the ladies could meet Noah so they could give their nod of approval. Which was also absurd. What, exactly, would she do if her two friends frowned on her new husband? Tell Noah she'd had a change of heart? Then do what? Go birding in Bolivar?

No, she'd made a commitment. She owed him, and the boys too. She glanced back to steal a glimpse of Noah's boys. They seemed determined to ignore her, which made her suddenly wish she could think of something to say to one of them.

What would Gertie and Bess say about the six boys? They'd had plenty to offer about Noah. Men, they explained, were meant to be managed. Last night, the three of them lingered over dessert and helped her compile a short list of thirty or so requirements for Noah Walker.

If she was certain he met those paltry standards, he'd be a good match. She might not get their nod of approval, but she had a list. As Noah guided the wagon along the road, she patted her pocketbook. The list, two pages long, sat folded inside, offering some degree of comfort.

Noah drove the wagon along the shoreline. The wind blew across the waves, carrying a slight chill, or perhaps it was just her own nervousness that made her shiver. She cast a furtive glance at Noah. When he turned to her, she looked away, hardly able to meet his gaze. Her heart thudded as they turned down a quiet street.

He stopped the wagon and set the brake. "You boys mind your manners inside the judge's office. I don't want to tell you twice. Hear?"

A chorus of agreement came from the back of the wagon. He jumped down, circled the wagon and reached for her. This time, his touch made her draw a sharp breath.

"I have a few questions before we say our vows," she said.

He nodded. For a long moment, he held her gaze. "Of course."

She tugged the paper from her pocketbook and unfolded the list. Her hands shook. She could hardly think. Her mind raced a dozen different directions. As her eyes prickled, she tried to coax a breath into her lungs so she could speak. Still, the words wouldn't come.

He grasped the edge of the papers and gently tugged them from her hands. She lifted her gaze, half afraid of what she might see in his eyes. To her surprise, a hint of a smile played upon his lips as he read the list.

"Number twenty says you get your pick of the side of the bed. How's that fair?"

He spoke softly, probably to keep the boys from hearing. Her face burned with mortification. She'd half-forgotten Gertie's suggestion about the bed. In her nervousness, Sarah had neglected to tell the ladies this was to be a marriage of convenience.

He looked indignant. "Seems we ought to get to know each other first," he said.

She wanted to point to his letter, where he clearly stated he needed a mother for his boys. No more. Instead, she replied with, "I agree."

He went on in a bland tone. "And then we can deal with all this other business. I run an auction house. In my business, everything is negotiable."

"Everything?" she whispered.

"Every. Thing."

She lowered her gaze. Each day of her journey to Texas, she'd imagined meeting Abigail. She'd yearned for her sister. Now, the entire venture seemed like a terrible mistake. To add to her misery, tears threatened to fall from her eyes. Her first day in Texas and she might weep. She tried to summon a shred of Bess's and Gertie's steel, but could find none.

Noah folded the paper. He lifted her chin to meet his gaze. Gently he brushed the tears from her cheeks. "I'm certain God puts people in our lives for a reason. I believe that. I will always care for you and cherish you. I'm not asking any of that from you. All I ask is that you care for and cherish my boys. That's all."

"All right," she whispered.

"You do that for me." His lips curved into a teasing smile. "And I'll agree to anything on your list."

Chapter Sixteen

Noah

He led her into the office of the Galveston justice. He stole a glance once or twice, marveling for the hundredth time what a pretty girl she was. It hardly seemed possible this lovely girl had signed on to becoming a mail-order bride. He considered asking what would make her leave her home and get on a ship to come to an unknown land and marry a stranger.

He also considered the question of her cooking. The need to provide meals for the six pesky, bottomless pits was his main reason to take a wife. Suddenly, he didn't much care if she could fry an egg. All he wanted in that moment was to say his vows before she came to her senses.

Sarah seemed as scared as could be. As they waited inside the office, he wondered if she might shake clear out of her fancy boots. Even a few of the boys noticed, eyeing her with mild concern. Mostly they didn't appear too taken with a new member of the family and regarded her with resignation or indifference.

Noah spoke to the clerk while the boys settled on chairs and benches. The judge emerged from his office and agreed to conduct the ceremony. Sarah grew even more pale. Noah half-expected her to hightail it right out the door and keep running all the way back to the ship.

Noah held her gloved hands as he faced her. This gave him the chance to study her features from close up. Her eyes were lovely, framed by long, dark lashes. Standing directly in front of her, he caught her honeyed scent and resisted the urge to dip his head to sample more of the fragrance.

He didn't dare. She already looked like she might faint any minute. When the vows were done, he lowered to brush a hasty kiss across her lips.

One of the boys snorted. Another coughed. A few murmurs of dismay followed. None of them would be keen on any sort of vows and least of all a kiss. At least they'd minded their manners till the end. The judge chuckled and pronounced Noah and Sarah, man and wife.

The boys regarded Noah and Sarah with a bored expression. Noah directed them back to the wagon, following behind as he held Sarah's hand.

From there, they made the three-hour trip back to Sweet Willow. Traveling in the wagon was a noisy business. It didn't lend itself to a discussion of any kind. To make matters worse, Harold and Dustin bickered for the better part of a half hour. Usually, Holden would keep them in line, but he was too busy scowling and pouting. Clearly, he'd expected a different kind of lady to step off the ship. Someone older and maternal.

Sarah was as fresh-faced as a daisy in springtime. He prayed the boys wouldn't run circles around her. She didn't look like she could hold her own, much less stand up to a passel of unruly boys.

Once they were on their way, she seemed to gain some fortitude. She didn't cower. She didn't tremble. Instead, she tugged a bonnet from one of the trunks, then put it on with a brief apology for the inconvenience.

"I'm trying to keep my freckles at bay," she said as she tied the bonnet.

"What's wrong with freckles, I'd like to know?" Dustin groused.

Noah narrowed his eyes and got ready to give Dustin a curt reply. The boys all frowned at Sarah in a way he didn't like. Not one bit. Before he could say anything, Sarah replied.

"Freckles look handsome on a young man. Everyone knows that." She offered the boy a slight smile. "You just wait, Dustin. When you're a little older, all the girls will tell you the same."

Dustin stared slack-jawed while the rest of the boys roared with laughter.

For the next hour, the boys teased him mercilessly, suggesting if he wanted to avoid freckles, maybe he ought to wear a bonnet. A pink bonnet. Maybe a blue bonnet with lacy stuff. More laughter ensued.

Normally, that sort of treatment would have left Dustin plenty mad. He'd tear up. Get quiet. He'd sniffle and finally his anger would boil over. He'd lunge at one of his tormentors, arms flailing.

Instead, he sat atop one of the trunks like he was the newly crowned prince of the buckboard. When the boys mocked him, he offered a triumphant grin and ran his palm over his unruly mop.

An hour from home, they stopped in a small town to buy some sandwiches. Noah bought enough to fill the boys' bellies so the meal could count for dinner. He added in a few dozen oatmeal cookies from the bakery next door.

By the time they arrived at the auction yard, it was past dusk. The boys had grown quiet. Sarah was quiet too, but alert as if taking in all the new sights. Driving past the auction barns, they came to Noah's private barns and home. The house wasn't much, but he'd have a bigger one built soon. He hoped she would find the place pleasing. Maybe even pretty.

He instructed a few of the boys to tend to the horse and wagon. The others he sent to unload the trunks and set them in the little spare bedroom by the back porch.

"May I show you around?" he asked.

"I'd like that. It's so pretty. Even though it's almost dark, I can see for miles and miles."

"I'm glad you like it." He offered his arm.

The feel of her hand in the crook of his arm satisfied something inside him. He'd wondered and worried for so long, not just about Sarah, but about the journey she would have to undertake. She was here now. Safe. Wedded to him. He breathed a sigh of relief and set his hand over hers.

They walked past the small house and up the path to the new construction.

"My home, our home, was never meant for a family," he began. "It was meant for the foreman and maybe a helper or two. I'm working on a new home."

The last light of dusk fell across the construction of the home he hoped to finish in a month's time or so. A house big enough for all of them. He intended to show her the inside when the floor was done. Until then it wasn't safe to walk around.

"When I bought the auction barn and the land, the house came with the property. The prior owner had already built a lot of it. Including the limestone exterior."

"It's beautiful," she said shyly. "It's quite large."

"We have a lot of boys."

She laughed softly.

He wanted to say something about, someday, once they were settled in the new house, having children of their own, but didn't want to say too much too soon. And the notion surprised him a bit too. In fact, he wasn't sure where it had come from. All he knew was he liked this girl, and could see himself an old man, with so many children and grandchildren that his new, large house would feel even more crowded than his tiny auction office felt today. The thought gave him a feeling of happiness like he'd never imagined.

The river flowed in the distance, a ribbon shimmering with a pale glow in the twilight.

He turned to face Sarah, wondering if she'd find the view as pleasing as he did. The question drifted from his mind. Even in the fading light, she was lovely. She'd pushed her bonnet back. It hung over her shoulders. Several locks of hair hung loose. He wondered what it would feel like to rub the delicate tendrils between his fingers. He slipped his arm from hers and leaned against one of the supporting braces.

"Do you believe in love at first sight?" He felt his lips curve into a sheepish smile. He wasn't sure where that had come from. He didn't think he believed in love at first sight, and yet he felt drawn to Sarah in a way that surprised him.

She stood with her back to him. He saw her shoulders rise and heard her sharp breath. Slowly, she turned to face him. "I believe you mean, love at first *glare*, don't you?"

He suppressed a smile. So, she wasn't a shrinking violet after all, or at least not all the time. Good thing. She'd need a little steel in her spine to manage a life with him.

"I glared?" he asked.

"You did."

"If I glared, it wasn't at you."

"It wasn't?"

"If I glared, it was at all those fellas falling all over themselves to say goodbye. And that was before they burst into song. Rascals. Singing to another man's girl. I was one chorus away from walking up that ramp and taking them all on."

"I'm sure they meant nothing by it." A smile tugged at her lips as if she found the whole thing amusing. Of course, she did. She probably liked male attention. What with how pretty she was, she likely received plenty of admiring looks everywhere she went.

His gaze drifted to her lips and the memory of kissing them in the judge's office. The kiss had been too brief. Here, in the quiet of evening, he could imagine pulling her into his arms and giving her another kiss. He pushed the thought away. He'd already teased her about true love and giving her his side of the bed. He shouldn't make any more untoward suggestions her first night.

She turned to face him. "What you've done is remarkable. I've never heard of such a thing."

"What do you mean?"

"Taking in six boys."

"Ah, well. Not really. It would have been remarkable if I'd planned it. The way it happened was so fast, I just didn't really think. They were in a bad way. I wanted to make it better."

"I think it's very noble. After my parents passed away, a lovely couple by the name of Becker took me in. At first, they wanted me because they needed a helper in their shop. I was just a child, but with my small hands I could manage delicate tasks like decorating candies and cakes."

He moved closer, wanting to hear more about her life. "But? What happened? Did you eat too many of their wares?"

Her lips curved into a smile that sent a wave of warmth across his heart.

"I admit I might have sampled one here or there. But the Beckers grew fond of me and I of them. They didn't need to treat me well, yet they did because they were good people."

"Is that why you agreed to come to Texas? Because you thought I was a good person?"

He expected her to say something light. Possibly something playful or teasing. Maybe because the moment felt intimate. They were alone, enjoying the fading light of a sunset on their wedding night. He wanted to know more about her life and to kiss her and a dozen other things. He had to admit he'd relish hearing more about how she thought he was noble. That was all right with him.

The question hung in the air. He'd expected her to tell him about what led her to come to Texas. As the quiet stretched between them, his desire to know deepened. Why would such a pretty girl leave Boston, or San Francisco for that matter? His heartbeat quickened. Was she running away from something, or someone?

She didn't reply. Instead, she bit her lip as if trying to think of how to reply. Fidgeting nervously, she avoided his gaze.

A weight settled on his shoulders. He'd been imagining all sorts of foolish notions when he really should have been asking more about why a girl like her would come all the way to Texas to marry a stranger. They hadn't even had time to exchange letters before she'd come. Why was that? He wanted to know.

"Why did you come, Sarah?" he asked softly. "Tell me."

Instead of answering him, her eyes widened with some emotion he couldn't place. Why would she respond to his simple question as if he'd accused her of some fault? She turned away.

A prickle of alarm moved across his senses. The question was simple. Her reaction troubled him.

"You're very pretty, Sarah," he said. "I imagine you had a number of admirers. Any one of those officers on the ship would have enjoyed time in your company. Why *would* you come all this way?"

His tone was a little harder than he'd planned, and from her expression, it was clear she'd heard the edge in his voice. In the soft light of the moon, he noted the retreat in her eyes.

"I came..." her words drifted off. "To be your bride."

She was not telling him the truth. He was sure of it. A growing unease threaded around his heart. While he would have liked to press her for a straight answer, he decided against asking again. There would be time to question her. He'd get the truth. Eventually. Over the coming weeks and months, they'd grow closer, learn more of each other and perhaps even trust one another. At least, that was his fervent prayer.

He'd hoped for a mother for his boys, but deep in his heart he'd dared to hope for a wife too. He hadn't realized that. Not until this moment. It was hard to admit. For a brief instant, he'd allowed himself to hope. It was better to view things in practical terms. Sarah was here for the boys, after all.

"It's late," he said matter-of-factly. "We can talk another time. I'll bet you're tired. We'll eat a bite and then I'll show you to your room."

Chapter Seventeen

Sarah

Nestled in her bed, Sarah struggled to open her eyes. She felt bone tired. The bed felt different somehow, the cotton sheets rough against her skin.

The sounds of people stirring and speaking wafted through her awareness. She tried to make sense of the words. Slowly, she began to understand. Talk of morning chores gave way to a discussion about a fishing hole.

Strange. Otto or Erna hadn't ever shown an interest in fishing. Neither even ate fish. Why would they go fishing when they preferred their schnitzel, sauerkraut and dumplings?

A dog barked. Another joined in. Dogs barking?

Sarah sat bolt upright in bed and looked around in confusion. Sunshine streamed through the window. She frowned, wondering why Erna, who kept her house neat as a pin, had only cleaned the lower windowpanes. And not very well either.

A realization came over her. A sad, stark understanding that Erna and Otto were gone. She squeezed her eyes shut and pushed the grief away.

Another chorus of barking greeted her ears. She opened her eyes and studied the room more closely. Her trunks took up the length of one wall. Two of them sat open. The contents didn't look familiar. Not at first. The memories drifted back.

Shopping in Boston. With Mrs. Penobscot. Setting sail on *The Sparrow*. Noah Bailey.

"Heavens," she murmured. "I'm in Texas," she yelped. "And I'm married."

A flush of embarrassment warmed her face.

The book that Mr. Perryman had given her, filled with instructions for the new bride, warned that the first rule of keeping house was to rise early. The first day as a married woman and she'd stayed in bed half the morning.

She knew it was due to sleeping so poorly. Last night, she said her prayers and asked God to forgive her for coming to Texas under what felt like false pretenses. After, she lay awake. She battled her conscience as she debated telling Noah how much of her desire to come to Texas was to meet a long-lost sister.

Last night, she unpacked one of her trunks to retrieve a few small gifts for the boys. Some books and trinkets which they'd hardly noticed. She'd also unpacked the dress she'd intended to wear when she met Abigail. It hung on a hanger and struck Sarah as far too fancy for Texas. She realized that now and felt abashed.

She went to the window. In the morning sunshine, she took in her new home in the light of day. The barnyard lay directly outside her window. In the distance lay the auction barns, but they appeared quiet, for now. This morning the activity concerned things near the house. She glimpsed a few boys in a chicken pen feeding the animals. Another boy sat atop a horse and spoke with Noah.

All the Bailey family was at work. Except for her.

Dressing hastily, she recalled the way Noah had gazed at her as they said their vows. His eyes held a warmth and tenderness she'd never expected. He'd lowered to brush a chaste kiss across her lips after they said their vows. She hadn't expected that either.

The memory made a tingle move up her spine. She touched her lips. Her first kiss. All the times she'd tried to imagine Noah Bailey, she hadn't pictured him so tall, so broad-shouldered or the way his lips would feel against hers.

She pushed the girlish thoughts aside. There was no time for silly romantic notions. Noah might make her heart skip a beat when he gazed at her, but she was certain he didn't return the sentiment. He'd made that clear last night with his gruff dismissal. After he teased her and spoken to her gently, he'd gone back to treating her like a stranger.

He wanted convenience, she reminded herself. Not a wife.

Fully dressed, with her hair pulled in a simple knot, she paused at her door, her hand on the knob. Her heart thumped with expectation. Last night she'd been too tired to dwell on her deception. She'd fallen into bed without so much as another thought about coming to Texas to find Abigail. She'd had a chance to tell him last night but had chosen to say nothing.

Now, in the harsh light of day, she'd come face-to-face with her tangled web.

She closed her eyes and thought of the way the boys regarded her with a mix of curiosity and suspicion. Resting her forehead against the door, she offered another prayer, asking for the Lord's guidance so she might be a comfort to this house full of menfolk. With prayer, she could right the path that had started on the wrong foot.

Drawing a deep, fortifying breath, she straightened her shoulders. Today she'd tell Noah about her sister. He could help her find Abigail, perhaps even arrange a meeting. The prospect of confessing the entire plan to her husband filled her with fear and no small degree of shame. What if he turned her out? She'd heard of marriages being annulled. What then?

Pushing her worries away, she left her room. Down the hallway, a door stood open. She crept closer and peeked inside. The small room contained bunk beds. All six boys slept here. The room was tiny, but tidy. Even the beds were made.

The next room had to belong to Noah. A large bed sat under a window. In the corner stood a desk. A fireplace took up the other wall. She took a few tentative steps inside, her heart quaking. This was her husband's room. The man whom she'd vowed to love and obey.

A wardrobe stood partly open. She would have liked to see his things. Her fingers itched to nudge the door further open. She wanted to snoop. No way of denying it. Several pairs of boots stood beside the wardrobe, most of them battered and dusty. One dark pair was polished and gleamed. Probably his Sunday boots. A pair of spurs hung from a hook above the boots, beside a coat.

A rack held several coats and cowboy hats. My, but Noah looked handsome in his cowboy hat. She smiled, took down a hat and studied it with curiosity. Men in San Francisco didn't wear cowboy hats. And the men in Boston didn't either, as far as she saw.

She touched the band gently, admiring the leather braid. Slowly and with care, she set it on her head. "How do you do, ma'am?" she murmured in a deep voice and chuckled.

Someone entered the house. Noah, from the sounds of the footsteps. A startled, inelegant sound escaped her lips. Grabbing the hat from her head, she shoved it onto the hook. She darted from the room and hurried down the hallway to the kitchen. Noah stood by the stove, pouring a cup of coffee in his hand.

"Mornin'," he said. His tone was neither friendly nor unfriendly. He took a swallow of his coffee, his gaze holding hers over the rim of the cup. "Sleep all right?"

"Very well. Too well. I overslept."

"Long trip. I imagine you're tuckered out."

"I am," she said, practically cringing with awkwardness. "Coffee's fresh."

"Thank you, I'll have some shortly."

She turned away from his fierce gaze and looked around the kitchen. A cast-iron pan with the remnants of a batch of scrambled eggs sat on a cold stove. Not only had she slept half the morning, her morning chores had been done by someone else. Heat crept up her neck. "I don't usually sleep so late. I should have been up to make breakfast or at least help."

He gave her a can't-be-helped sort of shrug.

A door slammed. Noah grimaced. A moment later the youngest boy, Josiah, came into the kitchen holding a half-dozen straggly flowers. He grinned and presented them to Sarah.

"Got you some daisies, Miss Sarah. Thought you'd like 'em. Please don't tell the others because they'll give me a bad time about it."

"How lovely." Sarah took the blooms. Josiah's sweet smile offered a welcome reprieve from Noah's stormy expression. The boy's dark eyes were the color of milk chocolate. A dimple notched one cheek, but not the other, giving his grin a lopsided quality.

"Where are the rest of the boys?" Noah asked, glancing out the window.

"In the barn, fixing to have a meeting." Josiah's eyes widened. "I mean, they're in the barn. Working. I gotta go help."

The boy turned and scampered down the hall.

"Finish your chores," Noah called.

"Yessir."

"Don't let the door-" Noah's words were cut off by the slam of the door.

Sarah wondered if she might see a sign of the man's temper. She held her breath, waiting, but Noah merely sighed and took another swallow of his coffee. He set the cup aside and folded his arms, regarding her with an appraising look.

She gulped. Otto had always said she was no good at concealing anything. The difficulty was especially pronounced when she was just a young girl. If he told her of a little surprise that he'd gotten Erna, Sarah always spilled the details. The same would happen if Erna tried to surprise Otto.

Erna and Otto both used to tease her about how she'd never last more than a quarter hour before blurting out their surprise. They laughed and called her their little nightingale.

Noah's eyes held a cool distance. None of the warmth of yesterday.

Her heart raced. She waited for him to lay out all of her transgressions, listing them off one by one and ending with the final accusation of coming all this way for the sake of a sister who was nothing more than a stranger. How he might know all this, she couldn't imagine.

He narrowed his eyes. "What are you running from, Sarah?"

Running? She drew a sharp breath. The flowers tumbled from her hand, dropping to her feet. She let out a small murmur of surprise and knelt to retrieve the blooms.

"Let me," Noah said gruffly.

He crossed the room, knelt to gather the flowers and offered them to her. His gesture was gallant. She was grateful.

The delay gave her a chance to consider the meaning of his astonishing question. She took the flowers from him, averting his gaze as she arranged them into a tidy, albeit drooping bunch.

He didn't move away, remaining just an arm's length from her. She tucked the flowers this way and that. The daisies gave her an excuse not to meet his gaze. His proximity, his stern demeanor along with his startling question, made her feel as if she too might wilt.

"I'd like to know if I should expect some fella to come looking for you," Noah said. "Do you have a husband back in Boston?"

She jerked her gaze to meet his. "A *husband*?"

He didn't reply.

It took her a moment to realize he was in earnest. He thought she'd come to Texas to escape a husband. The idea was outrageous. It was so far from the truth she almost laughed. The dark look in his eyes stopped any thoughts of laughter or even smiling.

He went on. "I've always assumed a woman agreed to become a mail-order bride because she had some ulterior motive."

"Well. I..." Her words trailed off. This was the moment to speak. She knew that, but her courage crept away like a thief in the night.

"I know you're hiding something."

"You do?"

"You're pretty – very pretty." His tone was more growl than anything.

Her face heated with embarrassment. "Thank you," she said softly. "I think that's a compliment, although I confess, I'm not sure."

"There are lots of nice things about you, Sarah. For starters, you're not vulgar." As he began to list things, he counted them off on one hand. "You smell nice. You wear pretty things. You're not an old gray mare, if you get my meaning. So, I have to think you came to Texas for some reason other than marrying me and taking care of six grubby boys."

She blinked. Had Noah just called her an old gray mare? Or did he say that she *wasn't* an old gray mare? Neither sentiment seemed particularly flattering. Not only was he comparing her to a horse, and an old horse at that, but he was insisting she was a married woman.

"Marrying two people is against the law," she said primly. "Are you asking if I'm guilty of..."

She couldn't recall the word. Her thoughts tumbled around her head in confusion. There was a term for this scandalous accusation. The precise word failed her. What on earth could he mean?

"Bigamy," he offered. "And yes, I am asking."

She lifted her chin and squared her shoulders. "The nerve!"

He arched a brow and took half a step closer. She refused to back away. If he was trying to bully her, she'd need to stand her ground and make it very clear she wouldn't be cowed. If men were meant to be managed, she wasn't doing very well with her husband of convenience.

"Let me explain something to you, darlin'." He jerked his thumb over his shoulder. "My boys have been disappointed by all sorts of women, starting with the ones that gave birth to them. I won't stand by while you waltz into this home and act like you want to be a mama to them. Not if you got some secret like for instance a husband who's on a ship right now, heading to Texas."

A breathless, disbelieving laugh tumbled from her lips.

He shook his head. "Trust me, you're not going to break *my* heart. That won't happen. But you might break theirs if you act sweet when you don't mean it. I took them in to protect them." His eyes softened just for an instant, but the hard look quickly returned. "And that's what I intend to do."

For a long moment, they stood toe to toe, neither speaking. She refused to reply to his outrageous accusation. Bess's and Gertie's words rang in her mind, the assertion that husbands were to be managed. She had to imagine neither lady had met as gruff and impossible a man as Noah Bailey.

Finally, after what seemed an eternity, he left the kitchen, taking his hat from a hook by the doorway. She waited. Listened. Hardly daring to breathe until she heard the door slam.

Chapter Eighteen

Josiah

Josiah ran to the barn. It had taken more time than he'd liked to finish up his chores. With a little luck, he'd arrive before things got started.

Holden always fussed about the latecomers on account of having to start his talk all over again. It seemed the older boy liked an audience and would enjoy the notion of saying everything twice. No. Holden always acted put-upon and griped about dawdlers and lollygaggers. The older boy seemed especially fond of those words, working them into his talk every chance. Probably because he noticed that Noah used the terms.

Shutting the barn door quietly, Josiah listened intently. He winced. The meeting had begun. Holden was already talking. Griping mostly.

Josiah crept through the barn and slipped inside the feed room. A rickety chair, with a busted armrest, sat in the corner, offering an out-of-the-way seat. Josiah crept along the back wall, lowered slowly, managing to settle without drawing attention to his tardy arrival.

With a smidge more luck, they'd never find out he'd given flowers to Sarah.

Josiah hadn't intended to pick flowers for her. The trouble was last night she looked sorta sad. He noticed it while she gave them the gifts she brought from Boston. The look in her eyes bothered him. Worse, he fretted that none of them had a gift for her.

After he went to bed, he thought some more and wondered if she felt lonesome. Seemed like that could be the problem. He recalled his first night at Noah's home. Noah heard him crying and brought him a cup of hot cocoa.

It tasted terrible. Really awful. Just the same, it made Josiah happy. He especially liked how he'd been the only one awake and the only one who got a cup of cocoa. It felt special. Josiah wanted Sarah to feel special too.

"She seemed mad last night," Holden said, pacing the length of the feed room. "That's good."

Josiah disagreed. She wasn't mad. Just sad. He folded his arms and kept quiet.

"It ain't either," countered Walt. "Grown-ups get to hollering when they're mad. I don't like it. The last folks I stayed with fussed at each other every night. After supper, the husband drank. Pretty soon he'd be drunk making a ruckus to raise the dead. Once he even broke a chair."

Josiah's own chair creaked underneath his weight. He glanced down, wondering if the darned thing would hold. If it broke, he'd crash to the ground and the boys would hoot with laughter, retelling the story for days to come. He shifted. The remaining armrest wobbled and tipped over. Josiah caught it in the nick of time before it clattered to the floor. He set the armrest aside, shot to his feet and moved away from the old, worn-out chair. Better to stand on his own two feet than sit on a chair with four wobbly legs.

"We don't want to make them fight," Holden said. "But we don't want them to get along either. Seems to me when a husband and lady get along, the lady starts talking about little ones."

A murmur of worry moved across the group.

Holden went on. "Even worse, when they get along, they hold hands and *kiss*."

They groaned. This time a little louder. Expressions of dread and dismay followed. No one liked the idea of kissing and couldn't understand why any man would tolerate that sort of thing. Harold, sitting on a stack of burlap grain sacks, clutched his middle, bent over at the waist and pretended to retch.

The rest of the boys laughed at his antics. Even Holden, who generally didn't approve of distractions during his meetings, grinned at his brother.

"So how are we going to keep them from getting along?" Walt asked.

"I haven't figured that out yet, but I'm working on it," Holden said.

Josiah kept quiet. If he could, he'd try to talk the boys out of their plans. Sarah was a nice lady. She'd given them books. Jacks. None of them had expected her to bring presents and it seemed the gifts should be taken into account and their plans to run Sarah off should start over.

Aunt Laura, the lady Uncle Seth had married last year, was nice too. She gave them gifts on Easter Sunday. It was the first time anyone had given Josiah a gift. He'd been so bowled over, he'd forgotten to thank her.

Laura was kind to all of them. And Sarah might very well be too.

Josiah avoided defending people, if possible. Not after he'd tried to talk the boys out of pulling pranks on poor Miss

Duncan, the teacher at Sweet Willow School. They hadn't paid him any mind.

For all of Josiah's arguing, the boys still managed to run that poor school lady off. Miss Duncan up and left Sweet Willow in a hurry. She was gone the minute school let out for the summer.

Times he thought his trying to talk them out of their plans made them more set in their ways.

Especially Holden.

"Someone's coming," Dustin said. "There's a wagon on the path."

They went to the windows and peered through the dusty windowpanes. A few muttered about the dirt, griping because they couldn't tell who was coming. They squabbled and jostled for position until one had the bright idea of opening the windows.

It was a struggle. Probably because the windows hadn't been opened in an age. Maybe never. Finally, the boys managed to scooch each window up a bit.

"It's Uncle Seth. And Aunt Laura. She's carrying a basket. So is Uncle Seth."

A clamor rose. Laura and Seth came once a week or so, often toting a basket of fried chicken or a fat brisket fresh off the fire pit. Aunt Laura was a fine cook and even better baker. If they were lucky, they'd find a pie tucked in one of the baskets. Whenever that happened, the boys would bicker about who got the biggest piece. Even Noah got into the fray. He'd demand a slice which always meant the pie needed to be cut into seven. Which everyone decided was tricky.

Josiah wanted to point out that Sarah might turn out just as kind as Laura. He said nothing, however. No one listened. After all, he was the youngest. The boys pointed that out every chance they got. None of them wanted to talk anymore about Sarah, anyway. They were too excited to see Seth and Laura.

Did she bring us some lunch? I love Aunt Laura. I think I'm her favorite. Nah, I'm her favorite. Shut up, dummy. Why don't you shut up? She's too nice to have favorites. I wonder if she brought ham and scalloped potatoes...

The boys grew quiet as a third person descended the buggy. Francine.

"Dang it all," muttered Walt.

A few of the boys groaned. They stood, unmoving, as if they might, with the powers of concentration, will away the sight of the girl.

Often Francine rode over on her pony. When that happened, she wore trousers just like the boys. Those times she made them call her Frankie. Other times, when she came with her parents, she wore a dress. When she wore a dress, she wanted to be called Francine. Some of the boys thought she was bossier when she wore a dress. The others claimed she was bossier when she wore her riding duds.

Josiah thought it was a draw. The girl was bossy no matter what she wore. End of story.

Today, Francine wore a dress. She strolled up the walkway, following her parents into the house. Her hair was done in a way that Josiah thought looked sorta pretty but wasn't going to mention. She turned towards the barn and scowled as if she knew perfectly well the boys were watching her.

"Duck!" Walt whispered.

"Get down," Holden commanded.

They huddled under the windows.

"Why'd she have to come?" Dustin grumbled.

"What a pest," muttered Harold.

The sound of Noah hollering for them came through the gap in the window, sounding like a thunderclap.

The boys scrambled to the door, crouching low to keep out of sight. No use drawing attention to their meeting place. They especially didn't want the attention of the mean, grudge-holding girl.

Any minute, Noah would holler some more, or come looking for them, or ring the lunch bell. Anytime company came round, they were obliged to visit and act sociable.

Silent and morose, they trudged home.

The meeting was adjourned.

Chapter Nineteen

Sarah

Noah was surprised but pleased to see his brother, Seth, and his wife, Laura. And Sarah felt a rush of pleasure at the prospect of meeting more of Noah's family. She and her husband might have quarreled their first morning as man and wife, but she still felt a deep curiosity about Noah and his kin.

She watched with interest as he greeted Seth with a handshake and a slap on the shoulder. Noah turned to Laura and gave her a kiss on the cheek, asking her how she managed to put up with his brother day after day. Without waiting for an answer, he leaned over to give the small girl a bear hug, practically lifting her off her feet.

"There's my girl, Francine." His voice boomed. "Pretty as a speckled pup."

"Uncle Noah, quit calling me that," the girl fussed at him, but wore a broad smile.

Noah then turned his attention to Sarah, inviting her to his side. When he set his hand on her shoulder and tugged her closer, she tried to relax and give the appearance of a wife.

"This is my bride, Sarah Bailey," he said.

The deep timbre of his voice held a note of pride which pleased her more than she might have guessed, but to hear her name paired with his stole her breath. *Sarah Bailey*. Of course, she was Sarah Bailey. Both Seth and Laura offered a warm greeting. Seth took her hand in his and welcomed her.

He gazed at her for a long moment with disbelief. "Never thought I'd see the day my brother took a mail-order wife."

"What my husband means to say is that we're so glad you're here." Laura folded her into a gentle embrace.

Sarah blushed. She still needed a moment to recover from the shock of hearing Noah call her by her married name. She smiled and stammered. Finally, she gave an awkward laugh. Both Seth and Laura gazed at her with a mixture of surprise and expectation.

"It's very nice to meet you," she managed.

Seth grinned. "How do you like Texas?"

"I haven't seen much of Texas," Sarah said. "I overslept this morning. I fear I'm not getting off to an auspicious start as a new wife. I hope Noah doesn't send me back right back."

Her stomach twisted. What had started as an attempt to say something lighthearted had turned into a partial confession. Her throat tightened. Laura seemed to understand her discomfort and set her hand on Sarah's, giving her a reassuring smile.

Seth chuckled. Even Noah regarded her with a hint of amusement.

"We said our vows," Noah said. "I reckon we're stuck with each other."

Laura shook her head. "Noah, those are hardly the romantic words a new bride needs to hear from her groom."

The young girl who had come with Seth and Laura offered her hand and introduced herself as Francine. Sarah said hello. The girl replied in kind, but Sarah couldn't help noticing how Francine gazed at her as if studying her intently. The girl knit her brows. Her lips parted as if she might speak her mind, yet she remained silent.

Sarah couldn't imagine what Francine might have noticed that caused such a response.

The men left the porch. The boys emerged from the barn just then and joined Noah and Seth as they set off to see the new construction.

"I should invite you in," Sarah said to Laura and Francine. "Please."

"We need just a moment to unpack the buggy," Laura said. "I always bring several baskets to feed this crowd of hungry boys. I suppose I won't need to now that you've arrived."

Laura and Francine made two trips to the buggy. An enticing aroma drifted up from the hampers, filling the kitchen with a savory smell.

"This is so kind of you," Sarah said.

"I might be from Boston, but I appreciate Southern hospitality," Laura said. "Francine, go set the table like a good girl."

Laura unpacked the first hamper. Francine remained in the kitchen doorway still gazing at Sarah.

"Francine," Laura chided. "Where are your manners, sweetheart? Why are you gawking?"

The girl blinked and shook herself. "I'm sorry. I couldn't help myself."

"What's gotten into you?" Laura asked.

Francine frowned. "Don't you see it? Look at her!"

Laura reddened. She turned to face Sarah. "I'm terribly sorry. I don't know why she's acting this way. Usually, she's the apple of my eye. Seth's too."

Sarah bit her lip, her mind whirring with alarm.

"You're Abigail's sister," Francine said. "The one she always talks about."

Sarah's heart leapt to her throat. She could hardly believe the child's words. Her breath caught.

Laura stared at Sarah, a jar of pickles in her hand.

A clock ticked somewhere, echoing down the hallway. Outside, the boys laughed and jeered. Noah called to them, offering some good-natured comments that drew more laughter from the boys.

Francine crossed the kitchen to take the jar from Laura's hands. She set it on the counter. Standing beside Laura, she folded her arms across her chest. "They have the exact same eyes."

Laura nodded. "My word."

"Francine is right," Sarah said quietly. "I'm Abigail's younger sister. I wasn't sure how much she knew about me."

"She didn't know. Not for certain," Laura said. "She was so young when her parents left her in Boston."

"I found a letter about that time. Correspondence from the orphanage. They left her because she was ill. I believe my parents always intended to return for her. That's all I know. I've been looking for her. My search brought me to Sweet Willow."

"How astonishing," Laura said softly.

"She's here in Sweet Willow?" Sarah asked. She felt sure her sister was here. Abigail had written the letter for Noah, after all, but she wanted to hear Laura tell her for certain.

"She is. Indeed. Happily married with children."

Sarah closed her eyes and swayed as a wave of surprise and relief washed over her.

Laura and Francine both began to speak at once and then took turns, recounting how they met Abigail aboard *The*

Sparrow. They unpacked the food and readied the table for the meal as they talked.

Francine told Sarah of falling overboard when the ship had docked and how Abigail had come to her rescue. Laura spoke of her and Abigail's continuing friendship. The talk of her sister warmed Sarah's heart. Hearing about Abigail pleased her more than she could say. At times, Laura's stories about her sister almost brought her to tears, especially the news that Abigail had twins.

Lingering in her heart, a heaviness remained, however. What to do about Noah and the unspoken words between them. How could she explain everything to her cynical husband? He was so protective of the boys and so certain she might wound them somehow. Just the notion of harming one of them pained her almost as much as his lack of confidence.

"I came to Texas hoping to find her. There was no time to write Noah to tell him of my hope to meet my sister. He doesn't know."

Laura looked perplexed. Sarah looked out the window, searching for the men. When she saw them on the other side of the auction barn, she turned back to Laura and Francine.

"Noah knows I'm concealing something. He thinks I have a husband back in Boston."

"A husband?" Laura said with shock.

Sarah drew a deep sigh. "He thinks I've come here to escape a husband and is certain the man is on his way to Texas right now. He told me in no uncertain terms. The man is furious with another man who doesn't even exist."

Francine chuckled. Laura fussed softly, telling her this was no time to joke. Francine grinned regardless. "Uncle Noah's jealous."

Laura shook her head resignedly. But Sarah noticed that Laura, too, had a slight tilt to her lips.

"I intend to tell him the truth about Abigail. Soon. I just need to summon the courage to explain that meeting my sister was part of my reason for coming to Texas."

Laura sobered. "Abigail isn't in Sweet Willow right now. She and Caleb took the children to see the seaside with Caleb's aunt."

"Oh. I see." Sarah sank against the counter. "Do you know for how long?"

"I don't know. Caleb's Aunt Eleanor has a cottage on the beach. They say it's a cottage but knowing Eleanor, it's probably a sprawling mansion. I'm not certain when they'll return to Sweet Willow. Probably in a few weeks' time."

Sarah rubbed her temples, sighing with frustration. A small, insistent throb sent a twinge across her shoulder. Suddenly, she felt very tired.

She'd traveled so far, first all the way to Boston and then from Boston to Texas. All the while she'd imagined the moment she'd meet her sister. Now she found herself in a terrible predicament and still hadn't met her sister. She wished more than anything she'd taken the time to write Noah about Abigail. Mr. Perryman urged her onto the next boat, and in her excitement, she hadn't questioned his suggestion.

The men's voices grew louder as they returned to the house.

Sarah went to the window to watch the men, seeking Noah amidst the group. He was tall. Broad-shouldered. He walked with an easy yet powerful gait. A shiver came over her as she recalled the man on the ship, how he cornered her and frightened her so badly.

"Does he have a temper?" Sarah asked quietly.

"No." Laura's answer was immediate and firm.

"I worry a little about poking the bear."

Francine snorted, clearly amused by the notion.

Laura waved a dismissive hand. "Noah does not have a temper."

Sarah felt some relief at Laura's words. Noah was head and shoulders taller than her. She could hardly bear to think of a man like him falling into a rage.

Laura nodded towards the band of boys as they drew closer. "Now that little Josiah likes to pitch a good fit every so often. It's always a bit of a surprise because he's a very sweet boy."

Sarah turned her attention to Josiah. The youngest of the group trailed behind the rest, a thoughtful expression on his face as he stared off at nothing.

"The older boys egg him on," Francine said. "That's why Josiah pitches fits. It's not all his fault. It's mostly Holden's fault."

"Maybe so," Laura mused. "Holden likes to think of himself as Noah's second-in-command. At times that doesn't go well. His brothers, Harold and Hugo, do as their told. They're sweet, cheerful boys. Quiet and always together."

Sarah noted the two boys walking side by side, a few paces behind Holden.

"Dustin can be a handful. His grandfather took him to an orphanage somewhere in East Texas. Noah's not sure where. He's fearful, always worried it'll happen again. He's a hard worker. Will do anything you ask."

"Except comb his hair," Francine offered.

Sarah chuckled. The boy's hair stuck up at odd angles giving him a decidedly disheveled appearance. He traipsed along, unaware or uncaring that his shoes were unlaced.

"And Walt is a kind-hearted, good boy," Laura said.

Sarah half-expected Francine to chime in but the girl said nothing.

"Some folks in Sweet Willow complain about the boys. They claim Noah had no business taking in a bunch of grubby orphans. Most of what they say about the boys is untrue. Or exaggerated."

Sarah wondered what Laura could mean. It pained her to think that people gossiped or spoke unkindly about the boys. She pressed her lips together as a spark of anger flared inside her. She was certain the boys didn't approve of Noah taking a wife. And perhaps they never would, but she still didn't want people to spread rumors about them.

Surely, the boys had been through enough.

"One thing's for certain," Laura said. "Every one of those boys thinks Noah hung the moon."

"I can only hope they'll accept me," said Sarah, "one day."

"Hm, well, you'll have your hands full, Sarah. That's for certain. But you won't have to worry about the man you married," Laura said. "Noah's a fine man. Just a bit of a grump. He's a little better now that he's taken the boys in, but he's a firm believer in finding a cloud for every silver lining."

"I'd like to find a way to get along with him, even if it's just an arrangement. We haven't been married before God, but still, I want to be a good wife to him."

Heavy footfalls thudded on the porch as the men returned to the house.

"Dear heavens." Sarah bit her lip. "Please don't say a word about Abigail. I need to gather my thoughts before my confession."

Chapter Twenty

Noah

By Sarah's third day in their home, Noah had to admit he liked her cooking. A lot. That evening he'd smelled the savory aroma a hundred paces from the little house. His stomach rumbled louder and louder until she called them to dinner.

The boys practically ran each other over as they raced to the kitchen. In just a few days' time, they'd learned the routine. Take a plate. Get into an orderly line. Wait your turn. Somewhere along the way, they'd decided on the line-up order. Oldest to youngest. No surprise there.

Holden always waited for Noah to go in front of him, but Noah liked to bring up the rear so he could keep an eye on the boys.

Standing in a line, the boys wore broad smiles as they waited to fill their plates. Sarah was telling them about the dinner she prepared, a savory roast, cabbage, carrots and dumplings. Her apron bore the marks of the evening meal, a splatter of gravy, and orange smear of carrots and three tan streaks. Noah wasn't sure where the tan-colored spots had come from. Maybe the cake sitting on the counter.

"Never heard of dumplings," Walt muttered, craning his neck, trying to see what she was talking about.

"I grew up eating dumplings," Sarah said. "It won't hurt my feelings if you don't like them. In fact, I want to know what you like and what you don't care for."

Dustin smirked. Noah cleared his throat to catch the boy's attention. He jerked his head and gave Noah a startled look. Noah narrowed his eyes to give the boy a silent reminder to be polite and thank Sarah for the cooking. He'd told the boys that they'd better mind their manners and thank her for the food.

The boy's smirk vanished. He nodded and looked away. Sarah began serving the boys one by one, offering a smile to each. Noah waited his turn at the end of the line so that he could make sure none of the boys squabbled or jostled each other in the tiny kitchen.

The kitchen looked like it had been struck by a small tornado. Dishes piled on the counter, taking up every square inch. Mixing bowls, pans, potato peels and eggshells littered the workspace. His wife had managed to use every single pot he owned.

Not that he had many pans. Everything in the kitchen was a collection of odds and ends. He'd had to gather up provisions and utensils in a hurry when he took in the boys. The same could be said of the rest of the house. Thank goodness Laura had ordered better amenities for the new house.

Sarah didn't wear her hair in the tidy style she'd worn when he first laid eyes on her. She looked a sight different. Her hair might have started out tidy that morning, but no longer. Strands of curled, honey-colored hair framed her pretty face.

Darn, but she was pretty. At night, he'd lie awake, his mind in turmoil about his new wife. What was she hiding from him? Over the last few days, his anger had faded as he watched her work tirelessly in the kitchen and around the house.

At the end of the day, she always looked plum worn out. He had to hand it to her. The girl was trying her darnedest to care for the boys. For that he had to give his grudging respect.

The way she spoke to each boy did something funny inside his heart. She had taken to the boys from the very beginning. He wished the boys didn't wear such sullen faces when she tried to draw them into a conversation. They were all smiles when she served up dinner, but the rest of the time, they hardly gave her a moment's notice.

The boys filed out of the kitchen until it was just Noah and Sarah left. She served up his plate but without the sweet smile she'd offered each boy. With them, she served the food carefully and lovingly, asking them if they wanted more of anything. Did they like carrots or cabbage or both?

She didn't ask *him* how many dumplings. No. With him, she smacked the food on the plate like she was mad at it. Each ladleful landed with a heavy thud. Half the cabbage spilled over the carrots. The gravy was doled out sparingly, a few drops here and there.

"I hope you like it," she said, her tone icy.

"Looks all right." His tone, deliberately indifferent, had its intended effect. She pressed her lips together, lifted her chin a notch and turned away.

"Cabbage, huh? Those little boys are going to be tooting up a storm."

She stiffened and slowly turned back to face him with her lips parted in surprise.

He shrugged a shoulder. "It's just a natural fact of life, Sarah. It happens. And they like to joke about it too. Maybe even a little bragging."

The color faded from her cheeks.

"You didn't grow up with brothers. That's why you haven't been around that sort of thing."

"No."

What was it about Sarah that made him want to tease her? He'd never been a boy who tugged girls' pigtails in the schoolyard, but, for some reason, seeing her pretty, blue eyes widen with indignation amused him. More than it should.

"You had a sheltered childhood, I suppose, being an only child."

She flinched. Dropping her gaze, she turned away from him as if his comment had wounded her. Maybe it had. Maybe she wished that she could have had siblings. There might come a day when the two of them would talk about their past. But not today.

He sat down at the dining table. When Sarah came, she took the chair to his right. They bowed their heads. Noah said grace, thanking God for the fine food and His blessings. The boys chorused an amen.

Sarah replied as well but in a quieter tone, still put out with him about what he'd said in the kitchen.

The boys ate like it was their last meal, devouring the food quickly. Sarah served cake for dessert, which scored points with the boys. Even Holden said a few appreciative words.

Noah wondered if she cooked fine meals just to impress them. Maybe it was because it was her first few days with them. Once she'd made a good impression, she might not make this kind of effort. He would have liked to ask but she didn't seem overly talkative. Not with him. She chatted here and there with the boys, but him, she pointedly ignored.

He was still thinking about the dinner the next morning as he prepared for the horse sale. He worked in the office above the auction barn. After breakfast, Sarah had announced she wanted to help, and he agreed. She sat in the office with Francine, tallying accounts.

Francine seemed quite taken with Sarah. Surprising. When Francine had come to Sweet Willow, she'd arrived with his sister-in-law. The girl had been a bit of a surprise to everyone. At first, Francine was shy, quiet and looked so frightened that Noah felt sorry for her.

Laura and Seth were newlyweds and preoccupied with setting up a home together, so Noah had offered to show Francine how to ride a horse. She took to riding and loved the little pony Noah brought her. Soon, she began tagging along with him while he did sundry errands. As her riding improved, she got past her shyness and reserved nature. They'd become fast friends.

That changed when he took the boys in. Francine, for some reason, had her feelings hurt. She told him he wouldn't have time for her anymore. She was prickly that way. So, it surprised him that she'd taken to Sarah. He half-expected more sullen silence.

"Mind taking the line-up to Holden," he asked Francine. "Bidding starts in an hour. He needs to have the Smithfield horses up first, the Rangel horses second."

Francine took the list from him, a smile playing on her lips, probably because Sarah had made her laugh a few times. Normally, Francine wore a look of contempt when she had to talk to Holden. The two were like oil and water. Of all the boys, she disliked him the most.

With Francine gone, silence filled the office. It felt heavy. Uncomfortable. Sarah gave him a furtive glance. She went back to writing down an account of the animals that had arrived that morning. He let his gaze wander across her narrow shoulders. A few tendrils had escaped the tidy knot. They clung to her neck. Impossibly soft, he imagined.

In the last couple of days, he'd come to regret telling her about his suspicion that she had a husband. It was a mistake. It was unlikely. She was shy, demure, not a woman who felt entirely comfortable around men. He didn't think she had a beau. And yet, she hadn't exactly denied it either.

"Dinner was good last night."

Her shoulders jerked with surprise. "Thank you."

"Don't think I've ever eaten dumplings."

He grimaced. He didn't like to boast about his ability to sweet-talk a lady, but usually he came up with better material than dumplings. Normally, he'd say something tender, or maybe flirtatious.

"My adoptive mother used to make them," Sarah said quietly. "She was from Austria. A far better cook than I am."

"You're not a terrible cook."

She flinched.

He chuckled. "No worse than me."

Silence returned. He got up and crossed the office to look out the window. The stands were beginning to fill. Each week, the crowd grew larger. Lately, he noticed many people came from towns that were an hour's ride or more from Sweet Willow.

He turned his attention back to Sarah.

She looked up from her work. "I wondered if you think the boys would like me to read to them. In the evenings, before bedtime."

"I don't know about that. You could ask."

She folded her hands in front of her. "I believe they have a plan to get rid of me."

He frowned. "Come again?"

132

"I've been told the boys are conspiring to make me want to leave." A faint hint of a smile graced her lips. "I happen to have a spy."

"Really?" He wondered if she was correct, but quickly realized she probably was. Aside from Josiah, the boys weren't happy about his taking a wife. Even with the improvement in the meals, the boys still sulked. He knew they didn't like the idea, but would they really try to get rid of her? They got up to some foolhardy plans, but this about beat them all.

He should find out more. Put an end to the foolishness. Instead, he found himself staring at her lips. He wanted to see that hint of a smile widen to a real, actual smile.

"Not one of them has heard a bedtime story," she said.

He shrugged. "Hadn't given that too much thought. Actually none."

She arched a brow, making it clear what she thought of this lapse in duties.

He hadn't gotten any bedtime stories either and he'd turned out all right. Course, that was a matter of opinion. From the look in Sarah's eyes, he didn't figure this was the time to point out his fine character. She regarded him with no small degree of accusation for not reading the boys a bedtime story.

He managed to keep from grinning. Barely. A bedtime story!

Most nights, he barely had the energy to take his boots off before collapsing in bed. Did she have any idea of what he'd had to do every day before she arrived?

"Go right ahead, Sarah. I'm sure the boys would love to hear a story. Especially your little spy, Josiah."

She swallowed and dropped her gaze. His conscience tugged at him. He wished he could temper his tone when he spoke to her. For some reason, she got under his skin. So much for newlywed bliss.

Before he could offer some way of apology, she spoke, this time her voice sounded soft, almost fragile, like she might tear up. Lord, he hoped not. He couldn't imagine making her cry. Would be worse than making her mad.

She looked up at him. "Did you tell the boys you thought I'd married before I came to Texas?"

"No. Of course not."

"I'm glad."

Irritation burned inside him. Regret did too. "Those boys have been hurt before. Their mamas either died or gave them up. They're just holding back a little. To make sure you're sincere."

She nodded. "Of course. I understand. I have to prove myself." The accusation returned to her eyes. "I'll do that. For the boys."

He went to the door, pausing to put on his hat. "I'm much obliged."

Unspoken words hung between them. He didn't want to bring up the subject of their quarrel. Not now. Not with an auction to run. He shouldn't have spoken to her so harshly. But she should have been straight with him and he was certain that wasn't so.

He was grateful for her efforts to be kind to the boys, so why was he gritting his teeth? The reason for sending off for a mail-order bride was to have a woman in the house who would dote on the boys. It was what he'd wanted all along, wasn't it?

Sarah had gone beyond his expectations with her care for the boys. She kept a small notebook in the kitchen with the meals she'd prepared. Under each heading, she had jotted notes about the boys, if they'd liked the pork chops, or the mashed potatoes. To his chagrin, she kept track of what the boys favored, but not a word about what he liked.

He left the office without a word. Maybe one day, if he kept up with the compliments about cooking and general charm, Sarah would want to treat him with the same care as she treated his boys. And maybe she'd come clean about whatever she was hiding.

Noah went down the stairs, made his way to the pens where the boys worked, pausing to give one final glance at Sarah. The office overlooked the auction barn and he could see her clearly.

She had her gaze fixed on him. His heart skipped a beat. His breath stilled in his chest.

The surrounding ruckus faded as he indulged in a lingering gaze. With a little distance between them, she seemed confident – a little sassy even. No, his wife didn't seem skittish now. Far from it. She regarded him with a look of bemusement. A smile curved her lips as she batted her lashes several times before returning her attention to her work.

He stared, slack jawed. Half the time, Sarah seemed intimidated by him. She seemed to fret that he might pounce on her and watched him with a wary eye. And yet, unless he was imagining things, she'd just given him a playful look. He watched a moment longer, wondering if she might give him another teasing, flirtatious look, but she kept her attention on her work.

He had to admit, if only to himself, a small twinge of disappointment. Still, she'd flirted with him. He was certain. He turned to head to the loading dock where the boys worked. "I'll be darned," he muttered, a smile tugging at his lips.

Chapter Twenty-One

Sarah

By the second week, Sarah's days fell into a routine. She'd wake before the rest of the family and serve a hearty breakfast to the boys and Noah. Lunch was sandwiches, ham or beef on fresh bread. Dinner, so far, had been a different dish each evening. No matter how much she cooked, the boys always devoured every bit.

She'd made three beef pot pies that evening. The boys cleaned their plates and asked for seconds. And thirds. After dinner, the boys thanked her and left to do evening chores. Noah got up and followed them. Pausing at the front door, he offered a word of appreciation and smiled. And then he was gone.

When he smiled at her, she'd forget how exasperating she found her husband. If only for a moment. As she tidied the kitchen after dinner, she found herself smiling too, however. The way his eyes warmed along with the rare smile pleased her more than she cared to admit.

A movement outside caught her attention. Two men had ridden into the barnyard. They dismounted and spoke to Noah. Whatever they discussed looked serious. All three men wore solemn expressions.

She went back to her work, scrubbing the baking dish she'd used for the pot pie.

When Noah called Holden over, she set the dish aside. The boy stood before the men, his hat in hand and spoke to them, answering questions. Sarah's throat tightened. Next to the men, Holden looked so young, so vulnerable.

Holden didn't care one bit for her. She knew that. When she'd tried to read to them at night, all six boys insisted they didn't care for stories. They'd practically run her out of their small, cramped bedroom. She recalled the look in Holden's eye. The hard, stubborn expression told her everything she needed to know. *He* didn't care for stories and had gotten the rest of the boys to say the same thing.

She knew that she might never win him over, but it hurt her heart to see him talking to the men. She could see that he was afraid. The way he fidgeted and shifted his weight made it clear he didn't want to speak to the men.

Noah set his hand on Holden's shoulder. They talked another five minutes. After the men had left, Noah said a few words to Holden and sent him on his way. Sarah wished that Noah would come inside so she could learn what the men wanted, but he busied himself with other work.

She yearned to go ask him what the men wanted. It wasn't curiosity so much as a desire to shelter Holden. The boy had looked troubled. That troubled her. After a little thought, she resolved to leave it alone. Noah liked to keep certain matters to himself.

A moment later, one of the boys came inside and appeared in the kitchen door. Walt wore a furtive smile. He said a shy hello and held a bottle of milk, the evening bottle for one of the animals in the barn.

"Something I can do for you, Walt?" she asked as she wiped down the counter.

"I'm going to feed the lambs."

"I see that. You're taking them their supper."

"Yes, ma'am."

She would have liked to ask about the men but refrained. Walt didn't usually talk to her much. Nothing aside from a few passing comments about her cooking, or if she wanted him to get the eggs from the coop. She didn't press him, however. The boys were reserved at best and didn't take kindly to many questions.

She carried on with her work and began drying plates. One by one, she stacked them on the shelf. Walt remained, watching her quietly. She could guess why he'd come. It probably had something to do with Josiah, her one and only ally.

"I already have breakfast planned." She showed him the bowl filled with dough. "I'm making sweet rolls. The dough will rise during the night while we're all asleep."

His brows lifted.

"In the morning I'll bake the rolls and fry ham for our breakfast."

"I heard something," Walt said, his tone tentative.

"And what might that be?"

He glanced over his shoulder, probably to make sure none of the other boys could hear, especially Holden. She wanted to tell him that Holden had just crossed the barnyard, heading to the corral. Their conversation wouldn't be overheard. No one would be the wiser. She kept that to herself, however.

Walt came a few steps into the kitchen. "I heard that you know how to make candy."

"I do," Sarah whispered. She took her tools from a nearby shelf and showed him the small bundle. Otto had given her the tools so many years ago, she hardly remembered receiving them. The tools were among the few things she'd brought from home. "These are the tools I use to make different types of sweets."

Walt studied the different utensils with interest.

"Is that a rolling pin?"

"It is. Is that the smallest rolling pin you've ever seen? I use it for rolling out certain types of chocolate." She pointed to the other tools. "I use the others to shape and decorate the candies."

"Someone told me you made caramels."

"I wonder who told you that?"

Walt bit his lip.

"Doesn't matter. Would you like to try one?"

He glanced over his shoulder, turned back to her and nodded, solemnly.

She took a small Mason jar from the top shelf and offered him one of the candies. He held the small chunk of caramel between his thumb and forefinger. After studying the candy for a moment, he put it in his mouth.

Resisting a smile, Sarah put the jar away. She made dessert every night and served it to the boys after dinner. The candy, however, she kept hidden. It was part of her plan. She hoped the boys would seek her out to ask for a treat. That would allow her to chat with them a little – not too much, of course. Except for Josiah, the boys weren't much for conversation.

"Thank you," he said, the candy bulging in his cheek.

"You're welcome."

He leaned casually against the doorframe, savoring the caramel. This was part of her plan too. The caramel took time to eat and she knew the boy wouldn't want to rush off. She kept busy, not wishing to make him feel ill at ease.

When he was almost done, she offered him a second candy which he gladly accepted.

He drew closer to speak. "You need to be careful, Miss Sarah," he whispered. "Mind you check your boots before you put them on in the morning."

She nodded. "I thank you. And I will certainly take your excellent advice."

"And under your pillow at night."

"Goodness." She knit her brow, schooling her features to keep from smiling. "Perhaps I should keep a list."

He shook his head. "No, ma'am. Just those two things."

"Thank you, Walt."

He nodded, put the caramel in his mouth and left. The front door banged shut and the house was quiet again. She gazed out the window. Holden pumped water into a bucket. If he'd been upset a few minutes before, he no longer fretted.

She recalled that the older boys sometimes worked at nearby ranches. Noah allowed them to take a job here and there because he knew the families and knew the boys would gain experience. Noah let them keep whatever they earned. She liked to think that was why the men had come to speak to Holden.

She let out a sigh as her own worry receded. She studied Holden as he filled the bucket, drumming her fingers on the counter, a smile tugging at her lips.

So far, she'd given a caramel to each boy except Holden. She wasn't sure if he knew about the sweets or not. If he did learn about them, he might avoid asking out of pure stubbornness.

After she finished the dishes, she mixed and kneaded the dough for the sweet rolls. Next, she made the filling. She covered both bowls and set them aside. While the house was quiet, she made a batch of toffee. The recipe was easy. She'd been making toffee in the candy shop ever since she could remember. The Beckers were famous for selling three different types of Christmas toffee.

By the time she was done, it was almost dusk. She tucked the pan inside a breadbox in the pantry just as Noah came inside.

He came to the kitchen. "Would you walk a spell?"

He'd never asked her to do anything in the evenings. Or any other time. She searched his eyes for a clue of what he intended. He regarded her with a matter-of-fact look. When she didn't answer, he arched a brow.

He glanced around the tidy kitchen. "You have time?"

"I've been here over a week and you've never asked me on a walk." A nervous laugh threaded her throat. "Why are you asking now? Are you going to take me into the wilds of Texas and leave me?"

He sighed. "Come with me."

"Who were the men you were talking to?" She took off her apron and hung it on the hook. Something inside her warned her not to ask, but she couldn't resist. To her relief, he didn't seem put off by her question.

"The taller one is a cousin, Beau. Next time I'll introduce you. He was here on business though. He's a Texas Ranger."

"What's that?"

"He's a lawman. He and his deputy need a couple good horses. I like to help him buy good horses every chance I get."

"That's nice."

He shrugged. "Not being nice. I'm a businessman, but I like the idea of a lawman having the best horse around. Especially if they're heading up to Sierra Mine. Rough country up there. Can't let the outlaws have better mounts, can we?"

She had a feeling there was more to the story. He'd spoken of the mines when he told her about finding the boys at the train depot. The term sent a shiver down her back. She wondered why Holden had been called over to speak to the men. Something in his demeanor persuaded her not to pry any further.

Besides, she had other issues that concerned her right there and then. Why would he want to take her on a walk? Was he cross with her?

Following him out the door, her mind whirred with a thousand worries. They'd come to some sort of truce over the last few days. They treated each other with courtesy but nothing more. He hadn't said anything more about his suspicions. She hadn't refuted them. Would he want to revisit their prior quarrel?

"Where are we going?"

"I want to show you the house," he said gruffly.

She parted her lips with a sharp breath. The house. Noah's men arrived at first light. They left a few hours before nightfall. Ever since he'd taken her up there the first night, she'd yearned to see the inside. Noah always said she needed to wait. It wasn't safe while the men worked on the floors.

His refusal felt like another snub. They'd had cross words that night. Since then, things had hardly improved. Her husband kept his distance, doubted her morals and motivations and, to top it off, wouldn't allow her inside their new home.

Now that he was about to show her, a giddy rush of excitement came over her. She'd never had a place to call her own. Never. Otto and Erna Becker didn't own their home and it still pained her to think how quickly she'd been cast out.

She tried to quell her worries. She was a wife now. Married to a man who wanted to give her a home. A man who wanted to show it to her on a summer evening as dusk fell over the land. Her steps lightened. Her heart brimmed with warmth at the sheer happiness of doing this thing with Noah.

As they walked the path to the house, she studied the structure.

The house was lovely. The front porch drew her eye. She could imagine flowerpots on the steps. A swing by the door. She could picture evenings sitting on the porch with the children and Noah too.

Since arriving in Sweet Willow, her thoughts were consumed with the boys and Noah. She no longer spent long hours imagining the first time she'd meet Abigail. From her first waking moment until she said her prayers and fell asleep, her mind was taken up by her new family and how to win them over.

Especially her husband. The man was kind and noble. But he was impossible. She stole a glance at him. His profile brought a smile to her lips.

Noah gave her a bland look, as if wondering the reason for her brightened mood. They walked up the steps of the house. He set his hand on the doorknob. "You seem happy."

"Because I am."

"You don't miss your husband?"

Not this again. She sighed and shook her head. The man was the most exasperating of all the males in her home. Noah seemed like such a gentle man. Yet he was willing to believe the worst of her. His cynicism and the anger behind his words that first morning hurt her feelings even now.

This evening, his tone didn't have the same sharp edge as the other day, however. If anything, his voice held the hint of a smile, and instead of feeling hurt, she considered how to give him a taste of his own medicine.

"Do I miss my husband? Let's see now..." She tapped her chin as if mulling over his question. "Which one?"

The corner of his lips twitched. "Let's start with the Boston husband."

"Him? Heavens, no. He was *so* tiresome. And my Philadelphia husband complained with every breath. The New York husband was the worst." She directed a pointed look at him. "Such a cynic."

"Reckon I saved you from those good-for-nothings."

"Indeed. Thank you, Noah."

After that, they walked without speaking. Twilight brought a quiet hush. Sounds drifted from the barnyard. Laughter. A taunt followed by more laughing. One of them called out an invitation to play a game of keep-away.

"I always tell my boys I don't like brawling." Noah spoke in a casual tone.

She blinked, wondering where this conversation could possibly lead.

"But if a man ever came along, making some claim on you, I'd make it clear you're not going anywhere. If it comes down to a fight, so be it."

Her breath stilled. A peculiar twirl of emotions fluttered in her chest. She shouldn't approve of brawling, his or anyone else's. Yet his words gave her a small glimmer of satisfaction. To think that Noah *would* fight to keep her. She smiled inwardly. Then she reminded herself she *had* no other husband. No one vying for her attention. No one to challenge Noah.

But still. Her husband was ready to fight for her and that was progress.

"I don't have a husband looking for me, Noah. I'm married to you and only to you."

He didn't respond right away. When he did, it was to push the door open and usher her inside. Stepping past him, she resisted the urge to ask if his invitation to see the house had rested on her reply.

He didn't trust her. She knew that. Until Abigail returned to Sweet Willow, she couldn't bring herself to confess. At least they had a tentative truce and that was the best she could hope for, for now.

When Abigail returned to Sweet Willow, everything would sort itself out. She was certain.

Chapter Twenty-Two

Noah

The cow, a young heifer, bawled mournfully. She'd been stuck in the mud for who knew how long. She might have perished if not for Walt's sharp eye. The boy spied the cow and had the good sense to understand she was in grave trouble. Noah made a note to thank him. Later. Maybe that evening. Not at the moment. Not when Noah stood right there with her, waist-deep in the muck.

Holden had waded in with him without being asked. That was his way, always trying to help. Always trying to prove he was a man. At times Noah fussed at the boy for taking unnecessary chances. Today he was grateful for the boy's help. Holden spoke to the heifer, soothing her, which helped more than Noah would have imagined.

"You boys keep the rope taut. Clear?" He spoke to Walt, Josiah and Dustin.

"Yessir," Walt and Dustin replied.

Josiah didn't say a word but nodded. Ever since the boy first caught sight of the struggling animal, he'd wept. His face was grubby save for the tear tracks.

The three boys waited on the bank of the pond, each boy on horseback. Their lassos stretched tight between their pommel and the heifer. Even with the tension on the rope, the heifer couldn't free herself. Exhaustion had set in. She could scarcely keep her head out of the muck.

They'd tried tugging her with the lasso, but that hadn't worked. Noah had determined they would need to try tying another rope around her mid-section.

He eased his lasso along her side and under her belly. "Can you reach it, son?"

Holden leaned over to try and grab the other end of the rope. The heifer jerked.

"Darn it," Holden muttered. He turned to spit. "I had it for a second. I'm sorry."

"That's all right, son. She's a little ticklish."

Holden grinned. "Yessir. Even with being so wore out."

"I'm going to duck under. When I go down, I want you to reach for the rope."

Holden's face fell. "No! What if she kicks?"

"I'll do my best not to tickle her. You do your best to grab the rope."

"Let me try."

"Nothin' doing. My head's harder than yours. And that's saying something."

Normally, Holden would have a quick reply. The two of them often bantered back and forth. The other boys might join in here and there, but only Holden could keep up. The others usually just listened in and chuckled at the exchange.

Holden pressed his lips into a grim line. It was clear that he would have dearly liked to argue but knew better. The boy wanted to be a man, but he understood when he had to follow orders.

"Ready?" Noah asked.

"Yessir."

"Keep talking to her. Give me to the count of two."

When the boy nodded, Noah let himself sink into the murky depths. Feeling his way along the cow's flank, he reached to the other side of the animal. He found Holden's outstretched hand and passed the rope under the cow. The cow didn't appreciate his efforts. Despite her fatigue, she kicked. Her hoof struck him on the side of his head.

Noah pushed up to the surface. He cussed and rubbed the side of his head.

Holden held the rope, staring in horror.

"It's all right." He wiped his eyes. Not that it made a bit of difference. Mud streamed down his face. "I didn't even see stars, Holden."

The boy muttered and shook his head in disbelief. Noah took the rope and secured it around the heifer's mid-section. The heifer bawled. The rope didn't agree with her and she struggled with newfound strength. She strained again, trying to escape the pond, to no avail.

"Just wearing yourself out, girl," Noah said, giving the rope a tug to assure himself it would hold.

He and Holden waded out of the pond, almost getting stuck themselves when they reached the bank. He untied his horse. As much as he hated to get his horse and tack filthy, he swung into the saddle. He wrapped the rope around his lasso and urged the horse back a step, and then another.

"Keep them ropes tight," he shouted.

The heifer heaved a step towards him. And another. Slowly, over the course of a quarter hour, maybe more, they eased the cow from her muddy confines. When she emerged, she stood on dry land, glowering at them.

"See the way she's looking at us, Josiah?"

The boy wiped his sleeve across his face. He replied with a tremulous, "Yessir."

"I believe she blames us for her mud bath. What do you think?"

Josiah nodded, a smile curving his lips. "I think you're right."

"You boys need to understand that just because she's tuckered out, she can still knock you down. Clear?"

The boys concurred. Noah rode closer to the heifer. She lowered her head and shook it, threatening him.

"Look at that ornery girl," Noah said. "Pretty sure that ain't a thank you."

The boys smiled and muttered a few choice words about the heifer.

Noah took charge of the ropes. He freed her from each lasso, one by one, keeping a wary eye on the animal. Thankfully, she gave him no trouble. When Noah finished, she wandered off, bellowing for the rest of the herd.

They rode back to the barn, the younger boys ahead, Holden riding beside Noah.

"Think this mud will ever come out?" Noah asked.

"Maybe with extra scrubbing."

Noah had hired a lady to care for his and the boy's laundry. She came once a week, but tonight he and Holden would need to do a little of their own scrubbing. He frowned at his saddle, covered in muck. Everything was filthy, but at least the heifer was safe and sound.

"I don't want you boys to give Josiah a bad time," Noah said.

"Sir?"

"He's tender-hearted. He can't help it when he gets tearful. Not a thing wrong with having a soft spot in your heart. Especially when an animal's hurting."

Holden nodded solemnly.

"Something else. I'd like you boys to pitch in."

"With what?"

"You already do plenty with the auction barn and the ranch, of course. But I want you to help Sarah."

Holden's eyes widened.

"It's nothing much. After supper, I'd like y'all to take turns clearing the table. Offer to wash dishes or whatever she needs."

"What about evening chores?"

"I'll have the others take extra chores."

"Yessir."

"And I'd like you be first. Starting tomorrow."

A flicker of resentment lit Holden's eyes, but he didn't argue.

"You're older and the leader. I depend on you to set the example. Just because you don't need a mama doesn't mean the younger boys might not. And just because you don't have fond memories of your mama doesn't mean you get to paint everyone with the same brush."

"Yessir," Holden said quietly.

They rode the rest of the way home in silence. Noah knew that Holden didn't relish the prospect of helping Sarah. The boy always took kindly to Noah's comments about him being the oldest, however. And the one to set the example. Holden was stubborn. He had a hard head, just like Noah.

Chapter Twenty-Three

Sarah

For some reason, Holden was offering to help her in town. He rode with her and Noah to the mercantile. Noah left them at the front door while he attended to some business. Holden rarely spoke more than a few words at a time. Today, the boy graced her with a comment about the purchases.

"We usually buy a bigger bag of flour, Miss Sarah," he said.

"What do you suggest?" Sarah felt pleased. While he kept her at a distance with his formal address, at least he was speaking to her.

"Twenty pounds. The shopkeeper, Mr. Morris, will give you a better price if you buy the bigger sack."

"Why, thank you, Holden."

The boy almost smiled. Sarah felt encouraged and made a point of consulting the boy on other matters as they shopped. The more she asked his opinion, the more he warmed to her. Or perhaps he simply regarded her with less scorn. Either way, she was delighted with the change. She relished the prospect of winning the hearts of each boy. One by one. Eventually.

The mercantile was well-stocked. Scents wafted in the air, spices, saddle soap, coffee. A couple of barrels sat near the corner, filled with pickles. Sarah and Holden walked past a counter piled high with bolts of various fabrics, bright silks, sturdy muslin and calico.

As Sarah selected items from her list, Holden carried them to the counter at the front of the store. There was a great deal that she needed to buy. She felt fortunate to have an extra pair of hands.

When they were a little better than halfway done, Sarah heard her name called from the store entrance. Laura, her face flushed with pleasure, hurried down the aisle with Francine trailing behind.

Holden turned on his heel, busying himself in another part of the store. Sarah noted the way Francine shot a glare at the boy. There were some bad feelings between Francine and Noah's boys, to be sure.

"I'm so glad to find you," Laura said, giving her a warm embrace. "I've heard from Abigail."

Sarah drew a sharp breath. "Has she returned?"

"No, they had to take one of the babies into Houston. It's nothing serious, but they're going to stay at Eleanor's home for a few weeks longer."

"Sometimes I wonder if I'll ever meet her, but at least she'll be here in a few weeks. I've waited so long to meet her. Now I can't help worrying."

"About what?" Francine asked.

"I don't know, exactly." Sarah's gaze drifted to Holden who stood by the window, watching something outside the mercantile. "What if she doesn't like me?"

"Of course, she'll like you," Laura said. "How could she not love you with all her heart? Oh, I can hardly wait for you two to meet. And then I'll have the chance to tell her more good news."

Sarah was lost in her thoughts, but suddenly noted the excitement in Laura's voice. "Good news?"

Laura nodded, her smile widening as sparks lit her eyes. "I'm expecting."

"Oh, Laura! How wonderful. I'm so pleased for you and Seth."

"We've been praying for a baby for so long." Laura set her arm across Francine's shoulders and kissed the top of her head. "God blessed us with Francine. We hope to have a houseful of children, God-willing."

Sarah smiled, her worry about meeting Abigail faded. Laura's bubbly happiness spilled over and swept Sarah along like a cheerful brook. Even Francine grinned.

"I can't stay and visit. I have to meet Seth at the barbershop. Just as soon as Abigail gets back, we must get the three families together," Laura said. "I can hardly wait."

Sarah agreed and bid her friend goodbye. She wandered across the shop, pausing to study Holden. He stood in front of a book rack, a farmer's almanac in hand. He paged through the book, pausing to look at a picture, then continued past, an especially thunderous look on his face.

He paused again, briefly perusing a chart, before casting the book aside angrily.

"What are you reading?" Sarah asked. "Anything interesting?"

She knew what he'd been reading, but suspected perhaps Holden did not. He reddened. Pursing his lips together, he shook his head. "Nothing, ma'am."

The store was quiet. One customer stood at the counter, talking to the shopkeeper about tinned peaches. Holden's expression shifted from anger to panic.

"Just something for kids. Not anything I want to read. I'm too busy helping Noah."

She nodded. "Of course. Noah depends on you for so much."

Eyes watering, he blinked and turned his attention to something outside the window. Holden swallowed hard. He jammed his hands in his pockets and kept his gaze averted. Sarah wondered if the boy might cry right there in the mercantile. She cringed inwardly.

"Do you know that I almost forgot cocoa," Sarah said under her breath. "And I promised Walt a chocolate cake after the cattle auction on Saturday."

"I can show you where it is."

Sarah turned back to the store. "I know precisely where to find the cocoa. The trouble is Mr. Morris keeps it on the top shelf. I can't reach it. Not unless I clamber up that rickety ladder he has propped against the wall. Seems like he'd keep cocoa on a lower shelf. I can't be the only woman in Sweet Willow who bakes chocolate cakes."

"I can get it for you," Holden said.

"A good thing too," she said airily. "I can't bake a cake if I've tumbled off a ladder, now can I?"

"No, ma'am."

"I'd have to sit on a chair and give instructions to someone or another. Who on earth would be willing to bake a cake for me? Everyone's so busy. Maybe Noah. I'm certain he'd be eager to mix up a cake batter. I wonder if my apron would fit him?"

Holden didn't reply, but by the time they reached the back of the shop, he'd composed himself. He climbed the ladder, retrieved the cocoa and handed the tin to her. They exchanged a look of understanding. He looked fretful. She tried silently to reassure him. Her heart squeezed with pain to think of how hard Holden fought to keep his pride.

She'd overheard Holden talking to Noah, trying to convince him that he didn't need to return to school in the fall. He was a grown-up. Noah agreed, but made it clear Holden needed to finish the last two years of school. At the very least.

Holden's eyes told of the secret pain he carried. She could think of nothing to say, nothing that would help, so she simply thanked him.

"I'm grateful for your help," she said.

"Thank you," he said quietly.

Chapter Twenty-Four

Noah

Noah woke early Sunday morning in hopes of slipping out of the house unnoticed. It wouldn't do to draw attention to his work. The boys would pester him with a thousand questions. They'd want to know everything. In the light of day, the topic wouldn't trouble them. The trouble came at night.

When Beau and the other Texas Ranger wanted to talk to Holden about the men, Noah had braced himself. He expected the boys to suffer more nightmares. Thankfully, there'd been none. Not one. He credited Sarah's sweet tender care for that. She doted on the boys even more than he'd imagined she might.

He moved around his room, dressing in his work clothes. Pulling on his boots, he grimaced. Sarah never looked at him with the same gentle gaze or asked if he liked the dessert that she served each evening. She treated him with respect but none of the warmth that she bestowed upon their boys.

He found her in the kitchen where she was already hard at work on breakfast.

"You're up early," she said quietly as she poured him a cup of coffee.

"I need to look over a couple of horses. My cousin, Beau, dropped by the other day looking for a pair of sturdy mounts.

I've picked out two. I'm going to give them a once-over before he comes by."

He took the mug of coffee from her, and instead of taking the cup with him, lingered in the kitchen. Sarah wore a simple muslin dress. Later, when they went to church, she'd put on something a little more refined. No matter what she wore, she looked pretty. He stole glances at her as she worked.

"The lawmen wanted to speak to Holden," she said casually. "Was that about horses?"

"Not exactly."

She pressed her lips together as she measured a cup of sugar and added it to her mixing bowl. "I don't mean to pry. I understand men talk amongst themselves. But the boys are dear to me."

"I know that."

Turning his way, she gave him a demure look from beneath fringed lashes. It must be a look she used to get the upper hand. To Noah, it felt like getting kicked by a mule. His breath faltered. He battled a fierce urge to cross the kitchen and kiss her teasing lips.

"If you don't tell me," she said with a subtle pout, "I'll just worry that's it's something terrible."

The lilt of her voice sent a rush of warmth through him.

"It's nothing to fret about, Sarah." His voice was gruff.

Undeterred, she added a soft, imploring smile which had the effect of disarming him entirely. He sighed and began his explanation.

"Beau is hunting the men who wanted to take the boys up to the mines. There's talk that the men, two brothers, Sal and William Montgomery, have resorted to kidnapping youngsters."

She stopped her work. Her coy expression fell away. The blood drained from her face.

"I haven't talked with the boys. I'd prefer if you not mention it either."

"Of course," she whispered.

"If it comes to a trial, they might ask Holden to testify."

Sarah nodded. He waited for a tear-filled response, but none came. Instead, she straightened her shoulders and offered a solemn, resolute expression. "I understand. I won't say a word."

He set his mug on the counter, thanked her and left the house.

The sun would rise in a quarter hour. Perfect time to put the horses through their paces. They'd arrived yesterday afternoon, delivered by one of his auction clients. Two fine geldings with strong hindquarters, well-suited to steep paths. And sturdy pasterns for rocky terrain. They'd do well for Beau and his men.

Noah tacked them up and rode each horse as the sun rose. As he suspected, both horses were fast, agile and responsive to every command. He'd paid a pretty penny for the horses. He told Beau that he didn't want payment for the animals.

It was the least he could do to stop the men from preying on kids. That's what he told his cousin. What he didn't tell him was that it eased his conscience. He'd had a chance to collar the men that day on the train platform but in the confusion, he'd let them get away.

If Noah didn't have a wife and six boys, he would have gone with Beau. He'd helped his cousin in the past, but those days were gone. Since he couldn't take part, he'd send the men on the best horses he could find.

By the time he was done working the horses, the boys were up, heading to the barns and pens to do their chores. None of them questioned his work. Holden gave him an inquisitive look but said nothing.

An hour later, they gathered at the little breakfast table. Sarah set platters of eggs, sausage and honey rolls on the table. The boys, noisy as usual at mealtime, marveled at the smell and sight of her cooking. Sarah set the food out with a smile playing on her lips, and when she sat beside Noah, they exchanged a knowing look.

Noah took her hand and blessed the food and added a silent prayer of thanks for Sarah. She'd come into their home and changed everything. An hour later, the family set out for church. It was a fine day with a bright, cloudless sky. Instead of heading to church with a weary heart, Noah couldn't help feeling pleased.

Going to Sunday service seemed to agree with his wife. Even though she'd only attended church three times, she already knew many of the parishioners. She always lingered to say hello while he waited by the buckboard. If she happened to bump into Seth and Laura, it might tack on an extra ten minutes before they could head home.

Seth caught his eye as he stood beside Laura and grinned. It was no skin off his brother's nose if Laura and Sarah visited. He only had Francine to contend with while Noah had a passel of rambunctious boys demanding to know how soon they'd get home.

When Sarah noticed he waited on her, she bid Laura a hasty goodbye and hurried to the buckboard. Noah helped her up. A moment later they were on their way.

"I'm sorry to keep you waiting, boys." Sarah put on her bonnet and tied the ribbons. "You'll be glad to know your Aunt Laura and Uncle Seth are coming for supper in a few days."

Usually, the prospect of Laura and Seth's visit elicited cheers from the boys. There was a little of that, but mostly the boys grumbled about Francine. Their complaints brought a smile to Sarah's lips. She glanced at Noah, a playful spark in her eye.

His heartbeat quickened. He tried to keep his attention on the horses but couldn't resist a second look. He had to admit he liked to see the way her smile tugged at her lips. More and more he admired her sweet smile and the way a blush bloomed across her fair skin.

"She's expecting," Sarah said in a tone that only he could hear.

"Seth told me."

"A baby. I can't imagine her joy."

He would have liked to ask her if she wanted one of her own. A few questions drifted through his mind. He would have liked to ask her a number of things, but even if she could have heard him over the clang of the wagon, the six boys in the back of the buckboard would hear too and they'd eavesdrop – the little rascals.

Instead, he waited till they got home. After he helped Sarah down, he left the horse and wagon with Holden and his brothers. The two geldings were gone from the corral which meant Beau had come while they were at church. Noah felt a little of his worry ease knowing the men had good horses. Sarah noticed the horses were gone too but said nothing and he hoped the next time they spoke of the subject, the Montgomery brothers would be behind bars.

Keeping Sarah's hand in his, he waited till the boys were gone to tug her away from the house towards the path that led to the new house.

"Let's take a look, Sarah. I'd like to ask what you think about the curtains."

"The curtains?" she asked, her tone edged with disbelief.

"What's the matter?"

She laughed softly. "Not a thing. I just never expected my big cowboy husband to broach the subject of curtains."

He frowned, feigning dismay. "I think about curtains all the time."

"Mm. Along with China patterns?"

"That was going to be my next question." He smiled at her. "I suppose a fine lady like you is used to all the plates and saucers matching. Not like what I have. We're lucky each boy has his own plate."

"I don't mind mismatched plates."

"I'll bet you grew up with fine dishes, didn't you?"

She didn't answer right away. A shadow passed behind her eyes. "My mother had a lovely set she'd gotten as a bride."

A moment ago, she'd spoken in a light, teasing voice. That had shifted to a tone edged with sadness.

"Seems like a sore subject."

"My parents left their estate to a nephew. Erna always said I'd marry one day and have a husband that would take care of me. They wanted their possessions to stay in the family."

Clearly, she was trying to speak in a cheerful manner as if the matter was of no importance. Noah heard the note of sorrow behind her words. He said nothing. What had started as a joke suddenly felt like something more. If her parents hadn't given her the things she'd grown up with and loved, he'd buy those things and more. The prospect made him feel a little better.

"I'm sorry that happened," he said. "But in a way she was right."

Sarah's brow lifted with silent inquiry.

"You have a husband. I intend to take care of you. Me and the boys are your family now."

She blushed and turned away. He wondered why his words would make her fret. Did she doubt him? He shook his head as the idea settled in his thoughts. He was accustomed to people believing him because they knew he was a man of his word. For some reason, Sarah held herself back. He knew she was hiding something from him about what brought her to Texas. He hoped to find out the reason. For now, he had other questions he wanted to ask, a question pertaining to his boys.

They went inside the house and walked around, inspecting the latest details. Sawdust covered the floor. The carpenter's bench stood in the middle of the kitchen. Tools sat on the shelves. The carpenter had finished the banister and doorframes. The doors themselves would arrive next week. Shelving lined the kitchen pantry.

Sarah walked around the kitchen, marveling at the spacious counters. The kitchen in the small house had only one window. The new kitchen had three, bathing the room in soft, summery sunshine. Noah hadn't given the windows much thought. It pleased him to watch Sarah's face light with happiness at the features of the new kitchen.

They went upstairs to see the boys' rooms. Another workbench sat by the window covered with an array of saws and hand drills. Soon, the men would finish and take their tools and the house would be ready for the family. Finally.

Noah leaned against the work bench, fixing his gaze on Sarah. "I'd asked Holden to help you with your evening chores."

Sarah eyes lit. "It's been lovely. I've enjoyed the company. And the help."

"I asked him because I thought he might not care for you."

He winced. The words sounded harsher than he planned. Still, she had to know that the boys grumbled about him taking a wife. He braced himself for her response, but Sarah didn't seem to mind at all. She ran her fingers along the windowsill.

"He didn't care for me," she said. "But we get along fine now."

"Seems odd."

She knit her brow. "There's nothing odd about it."

"He started helping you just a few days ago. He griped about the notion of being stuck in the kitchen. Yet, he's told the other boys he intends to help you every night."

"Hm. What's odd about that?"

"Are you making him do something unpleasant, something other than wash dishes?"

She blinked. The color drained from her face. "What a question."

"I'm asking because the first couple evenings I saw him leave the kitchen with tears in his eyes. Now he's a little happier about matters. I still wonder what got him upset to begin with."

"Noah, I'm not sure what to say," she spoke softly.

"How about the truth? Holden's not one to tear up. Why was he upset?"

"I promised I wouldn't tell you." Her voice was scarcely more than a whisper.

He folded his arms and stared at her in disbelief. "You're keeping another secret from me? About Holden?"

She straightened and lifted her chin a notch. "It's not for me to say. Not after I promised him. He begged me. You'll just have to trust that I have his best interests in mind."

"How is it possible that Holden went from disliking you to sharing a secret with you?"

"Ask him."

"I *did* ask him. He wouldn't tell me."

"I'm sorry. But I won't tell you either."

"You don't sound sorry," Noah muttered. "Not one bit."

Sarah turned away as if to show the subject was closed. He wanted to remind her of the vows they'd said. Especially the part about love and obey.

She peered out the window, tapping the pane. "I can picture some roses down there. Yellow roses."

He grumbled a few choice words that culminated with a growl deep in his chest.

"Pink would be lovely too," she murmured.

He shook his head with dismay. How was it possible his wife and son shared a secret? A secret they wouldn't tell him? When he first glimpsed Holden hurry from the house with a distraught expression, Noah's protectiveness sprang to life. He debated what to do about the apparent family strife.

At first, he'd decided to let it go. It was important that Holden and Sarah work out their differences. But then the worry burrowed under his skin. When Holden started smiling and acting happy about things, he worried a little less. Still, the entire matter galled him. He wanted to know, how in the space of just a few days, Holden and Sarah had gone from not getting along to getting along just fine and dandy.

167

Sarah might be right. He'd need to trust her. Just the same, he wasn't pleased about it.

He went to the doorway, pausing to ask, "Want to see my room?"

"That would be nice."

He tried to hide his smug smile. She might be a little surprised when she saw it. That was his guess.

She followed him down the hallway to the large bedroom on the other side. He stood by the window and watched as she perused the details, a smile playing on her lips. "It's lovely," she said. "Why, it's twice the size of the room you have now. Maybe more."

He waited.

"Where is my room?" she asked. "I don't believe you've shown me."

"This is your room."

She whirled to face him, her lips forming a small oval of wordless surprise.

"We're married, Sarah."

"You wrote about a marriage of convenience. I'm certain."

"I did, in the beginning. I didn't expect a lady who already had a horde of husbands, though. I figured you'd be fine sharing a room."

His joke fell flat. Usually, a comment like that would earn him a smile, but not today. There were other times when she seemed almost fearful of him and now that he recalled her trepidation, he regretted his words.

"We didn't say our vows in church, Noah."

"I know that."

She stood before the window with the sunshine lighting her narrow frame. She folded her arms across her chest as if hugging herself. The gesture made her look small and vulnerable. He rubbed the back of his neck with discomfort. Anytime they had a conversation, it seemed to end with bad feelings. He'd never had trouble flirting and sweet-talking, not till he got married.

"What I should say is that I'd like to share a room with you, Sarah. I hoped you might feel the same way."

She nodded. He wasn't sure what to make of that. He forged ahead, trying to make sense of her response. "At times you seem a little skittish. Like you might be a little afraid of me."

"It's nothing. Just a little fretfulness."

"Has anyone ever hurt you?"

His heart squeezed as he waited for her reply.

Finally, she spoke in a hushed tone. "A man on the ship treated me roughly."

He recalled the officers on the ship and the captain's words about an incident. At the time, he'd dismissed the comment. Now he wished he'd asked more. He grimaced as he raked his fingers through his hair. A rush of protectiveness came over him. He curled his fingers into a fist. "He hurt you?"

"He frightened me."

Noah closed the distance between them, stopping a pace or two from her. She looked so fragile. He wanted to pull her into his embrace, to make her bad memories go away. "I would never hurt you. Or frighten you."

She kept her gaze averted. "I've never been married, Noah. I've never been courted."

"I understand. I'm sorry I said all that. I couldn't imagine how you didn't have a hundred fellas lining up for you."

Her shoulders sank a notch as she took in his words and her relief made him wish he hadn't waited so long to apologize. She was hiding something from him, but he felt certain it wasn't another fellow.

She turned to face him, giving him a solemn, assessing look. "You remember the day we said our vows?"

"Sarah..." He said gently. Unable to resist, he cupped her jaw and stroked his thumb over her cheek. "Of course."

She closed her eyes and leaned into his hand. "That was the first time I'd ever been kissed."

A small wave of satisfaction washed over him. Sarah could have had any fella she wanted, but she'd agreed to be his. And she'd never kissed anyone but him. He wanted to wrap his arms around her and never let go.

He lowered, wondering if she would retreat or allow him to kiss her. He paused. "I kissed you in front of all those boys. The first time."

When she didn't withdraw, he realized that for the first time since getting married, he and Sarah were acting like husband and wife. He hadn't understood how much he yearned to touch her. How much he needed to be close to her. The awareness came as a bit of a shock to him.

"Yes." She smiled and went on in a gentle, teasing tone. "It was a kiss of convenience."

He brushed his lips across hers. "Maybe I should kiss you again."

"I'm not sure if that's prudent," she whispered.

"Neither is sleeping in the same room."

"Mmm..."

"You've got a week to think about it. A week before we move in."

"I'll give it some thought."

He growled softly. "You'd *better* let me sleep in the same room."

She drew back. Her eyes widened. "And why?"

Tugging her back into his embrace, he kissed the corner of her mouth. "Otherwise, one of us will have to bunk with a bunch of smelly boys."

She parted her lips. Maybe so she could sass him. Yes – probably. He noted the glint in her eye but silenced her response. His lips found hers as he drew her into his arms. Her kiss was soft, sweet and tasted of everything he'd ever hoped for.

Chapter Twenty-Five

Holden

There was something about the kitchen that made him feel better, Holden noted. When Noah first asked him to help Sarah, he'd balked. The first couple of evenings had been the worst. She'd made him haul water to wash dishes and sit at the counter while she washed the dishes. She scrubbed the dinner plates while he read. Or tried to read.

The first night, he sat on the stool, refusing to even try.

The second night, she sat beside him while the dishes soaked in the suds. They took turns reading pages aloud. By the end, he was so mad he could spit. Tears welled in his eyes and to his dismay, he thought Noah had noticed his tears as he left the house.

The third night was different. Instead of reading some baby book that Sarah had owned since she was a girl, they read something different. A story about a young cowboy who stalked a couple of cattle rustlers across the Texas plains.

It was sort of interesting. Better than a girl's story anyway.

It probably helped that the cowboy's name was Landon and the same age as Holden. Even better, that evening's reading ended right when Landon was sneaking up on the bad guys. At night. And With nothing more than a pencil and a ball of twine. The pencil wasn't even sharp, which Holden figured didn't bode well for Landon.

The next day, Holden wondered how things might turn out. His thoughts ventured to different possibilities. The boy was up against terrible odds what with just one of him trying to take on two outlaws, grown men at that.

Holden came to the kitchen a quarter hour early that evening. "I think I know what he's going to do with the twine."

"Do you?" Sarah asked.

She worked on a pan of something that smelled delicious. Holden came to her side and watched with fascination. The dilemma of Landon drifted from his mind as she sliced the contents of the pan into small squares. The sweet aroma made his mouth water.

"What is that?"

"Caramel. Would you like one?"

"Yes, ma'am."

She offered him the corner piece and continued working.

"You made those today?" he mumbled around the chunk of candy.

"I did. It's not easy making dinner for eight people with such a small stove, but I managed."

Holden turned his attention to the stove. It wasn't really a proper stove, just something that had fit the narrow kitchen. Holden had lived in several houses and this stove was by far the smallest he'd ever seen. For the first time, he noticed that it only had two burners. Usually, dinner used several pans which meant Sarah likely needed to switch pots around. He'd never given it much thought, but it made him appreciate the candy that much more.

When she finished, she covered the tray with a tea towel and wiped her hands on her apron.

"What are you going to do with the rest of them?"

"Wrap them in wax paper. Your Aunt Laura and Uncle Seth are coming tomorrow for supper. I want to send some with her."

Holden wrinkled his nose. He didn't like to imagine Francine enjoying the caramels, candy he felt belonged more to him and the boys and Noah too. Still, he was grateful he got one. While he wanted to keep the caramels for his family, he was secretly pleased that he'd been given one before the other boys.

He settled on the chair by the counter and began to read as best as he could with the caramel lodged in his cheek. When he got to the bottom of the page, Sarah stopped him.

"Why is it that you can read this but struggle other times?"

A few days ago, her question would have angered him. Not today. He knew she'd written the story just for him. She'd used easy words. Instead of writing in cursive like the teacher at the Sweet Willow school, she'd printed her words neatly. And while the words were easy, the story wasn't babyish. There was another big difference. Best of all, none of his brothers were around to taunt his poor reading skills.

"Miss Duncan used to make me read aloud. I'd get sorta nervous and mess up and stutter. It got so bad that I'd start sweating every time we opened our readers. I was one of the oldest in class, but she gave me a book for the youngest kids. I'd read about kittens or some nonsense. She'd correct me every single time I made a mistake. My brothers used to laugh. You don't say anything. You just let me go on and then when I realize the story doesn't make sense, I can go back and read it right."

Sarah pursed her lips and nodded slowly like she was thinking over his words.

He was grateful that she didn't seem to feel sorry for him. The last thing he wanted was her sympathy. That would be worse than when the boys laughed at all his mistakes.

"I'm glad for the story, too," he added. "Glad it's not about kittens."

Sarah smiled. "I promise not to write about kittens."

"I'm much obliged." His gaze drifted to the pan of candies.

"You can have a candy, Holden." She arched a brow. "As soon as you finish the last page."

He grumbled good-naturedly and continued reading. When he took his time, he did a little better. It was hard not to hurry though. He wanted to be done so he could pop the caramel in his mouth. Despite his eagerness, he forced himself to be slow and careful.

To his dismay, his theory about Landon's plan was wrong. The boy did not manage to outsmart the ruffians. Instead, they caught him. To add insult to injury, they used his own twine. Holden shook his head with disgust as he finished the page. When he got to the bottom, he turned it over and found the back blank.

"Where's the rest?" he demanded.

"The rest of what?" Sarah leaned her hip against the counter, savoring one of her caramels.

"Why, the rest of the story of course."

She tapped her forehead.

"Aw, c'mon. That's not right. You can't end it there. You can't just leave him tied up by the campfire while those bad guys make fun of him calling him names and whatnot."

"Maybe things will work out for him."

"Maybe?" Holden got up from the stool and jammed his hands into his pockets. "How am I supposed to go to sleep tonight thinking about poor Landon tied up while those bad guys rile him up?"

"I don't know how you'll manage."

A smile tugged at her lips.

"You're not going to do something mean to him, are you?"

"Like put a toad in his boot?"

Try as he might, Holden couldn't keep a smile from curving across his lips. "That wouldn't be all bad. I'm more worried about serious harm. Something dire. Something permanent."

Sarah frowned and drew back in dismay. "You can rest easily tonight, Holden, nothing terrible will happen to Landon."

"Thank goodness."

"Nothing that would cause pain."

"All right. That's good."

"Or a rash of some sort. No cooties." She tapped her chin as she mulled over other possible means of tormenting poor Landon. Brightening, she added, "absolutely *no* earwigs."

Holden drew a sharp breath. Earwigs? Were those the critters that crawled in your ear while you were sleeping? The things she listed sounded terrible indeed. Far worse than frogs or toads or the sort of tricks he relied on.

How could such a nice, sweet-looking lady like Sarah even come up with such notions? He fretted, trying to imagine what she might have in store for poor Landon. He put the caramel in his mouth and regarded Sarah appraisingly. Rethinking his prior opinion, he granted her a measure of new respect.

Chapter Twenty-Six

Sarah

Lamplight flickered across the paper and the small table. Sarah sat in the corner of her small room, working on the conclusion of the story. She couldn't help smiling. Holden liked to think he knew what would happen next. Not once, in over a dozen evenings, had he predicted the next twist in Landon's tale.

A noise drew her from her writing. She set the pen down and rose from her chair. Pausing in the doorway, she listened intently.

That morning, Walt had woken with an upset tummy. She made him chicken soup, convinced him to stay in bed to rest and tended to him throughout the day. At first, he'd grumbled. As the day wore on, he seemed to enjoy the extra attention. By dinnertime he seemed better, but she still worried he might not be well and that his tummy troubles might be catching.

Clad only in her gown, she crept down the darkened hallway. When she reached the boys' bedroom, she stopped and waited. She didn't want to go inside the room. The last time she checked on a boy, she'd woken him. He'd began chatting amiably. In an instant, two more boys woke, joining the predawn conversation. Which woke Noah, who emerged from his bedroom, growling like a bear.

The boys slept. The only noise coming from the room was the sound of sleepy sighs. She gave a silent prayer of thanksgiving that Walt rested peacefully. After a few moments, she assured herself that all was well and returned to her room.

The sound of footsteps greeted her as she drew near her door. She held her breath. A wave of embarrassment warmed her skin as she realized she didn't even have her wrapper. Noah had never seen her in her gown.

He stepped from the shadows and stopped in front of her bedroom door. Lamplight from her room lit his face, showing his expression of concern.

"What's wrong?"

"Nothing. I thought I heard a noise and wanted to make sure Walt wasn't ailing or troubled."

He knit his brow. "Another nightmare?"

"No. He's fine. Sleeping. I think one of them mumbled in his sleep."

Noah's taut features relaxed. "Good. They haven't had a nightmare since you've come. Thank you for going to them. You woke before I did."

"It's no trouble. I had woken earlier."

"What are you doing?" He folded his arms and leaned against the doorframe. "It's five thirty in the morning. You should be sleeping."

His gaze wandered from her eyes to the lace collar of her gown. She felt a blush bloom along her neck and drift to her cheeks. It was absurd. Or so she tried to tell herself. She needn't feel awkward. Noah was her husband. She was his wife. In a few days' time, they'd share a bedroom. Still, she couldn't help feeling a little shy. She swallowed hard, trying to dislodge the lump in her throat.

A corner of his mouth tipped upwards. "Are you going to tell me what you're doing, Sarah? Or do I need to guess?"

"I couldn't sleep." She slipped past him, seeking refuge in her room and sank in the chair by the table. "I'm writing."

To her surprise, he stepped inside her room. He wore a pair of pajamas that looked identical to what the boys all wore. The sight of Noah dressed like the boys might have amused her another time but not when he stood in the middle of her room. He was head and shoulders taller than she was. The room, which was small to begin with, suddenly seemed even smaller.

"Are you writing a letter?" he asked. "In the middle of the night?"

"I am not. I'm writing a little story is all. Just something for my amusement."

He gave her a look of disbelief. Clearly, he didn't believe she'd gotten up to write a story. Not in the dead of night. Did he still believe she had a beau? Surely, he didn't. Especially after the kiss he'd given her in the new house. The memory of that kiss had returned to her a hundred times in the last few days. He hadn't mentioned a word of it. Every so often he smiled at her in a way that warmed her heart and made her wonder if he thought of it as often as she did.

"You're telling me that you got up in the night to write a story and not a letter?" He craned his neck to peer at her writing but didn't venture closer to see for himself.

"No letter. Not yet, but I will." She held up a letter from Bess and Gertie that had come that morning. "I need to send a reply to the two ladies I befriended on the ship, Bess and Gertie. They are sisters and spending the summer on Bolivar Island..."

Her words died off. To her shock, Noah sauntered to the side of her bed and stretched out his long frame on the unmade bed. He reclined against the pillow. Cupping his hands behind his head, he regarded her with interest as if Bess and Gertie were a topic he dearly wished to discuss. He looked absurd in her little bed. It was far too short. Too narrow as well, but that didn't stop him from settling in with a contented sigh.

"Go on."

"Well…" Her thoughts spun. "Pardon me?"

"Bolivar Island," he prompted. "Bess and Gertie."

"Ah, yes. They're visiting the island to see the birds. They like birds. A great deal. So, so many birds."

His lips quirked. "Birds are nice."

"Indeed."

"I'm glad you had friends on the boat. *Lady* friends."

She didn't miss the emphasis he placed on the word "lady".

"They were very kind to me," she said. "The officers were as well, but I think that Bess and Gertie provided as much protection as the ship's officers. I might add that their last name is Payne. They make a point of telling everyone. And it was quite fitting."

Noah smiled. His white teeth flashed against the rough burr of his short beard. He only shaved a few times a week. Sarah thought him even more handsome when he neglected his razor.

Neither spoke. Silence drifted between them. He kept his gaze fixed firmly on her, making her heart flutter inside her chest. She wasn't quite sure what to do about her husband lying in her bed. He seemed content to remain, which left the question of where she would sleep when it came time to lie down.

By now it must be near morning. Perhaps she wouldn't return to her bed. She eyed the soft blankets wistfully. Earlier, she'd woken up with a surprise ending for Holden's story. Excitement had sparked a hundred other thoughts, chasing away any notion of rest. Now that she was done, she wished she could catch a little more sleep before the new day dawned.

Outside her window, a dove cooed. She glanced past the lace curtains to see a thin thread of crimson burning across the horizon. The dove gave another soft, melancholy sound.

"That's a mourning dove," Noah said quietly. "Your friends, Bess and Gertie, likely hear them down on Bolivar Island. The noisy gulls might drown them out, the rascals."

She smiled. "I'll ask them when I reply to their letter."

He crooked his finger, beckoning. "Come here."

What could he mean? She hardly dared to breathe as she considered his words.

"C'mon, Sarah," he whispered. "It's almost dawn. We just have a short while. Let's spend it together."

"Together?"

He nodded solemnly although she was certain if the light were better, she'd see a playful glint in his eye. "Together. I won't bite. We might as well get used to that together stuff."

He motioned with his fingers.

He wanted her to lie next to her. The suggestion didn't strike her as flirtatious, or even playful, but the idea of being so close to him unnerved her. He'd kissed her. Twice. Somehow that was nothing like what he was proposing now.

She rose unsteadily and crossed the room. He tsked and frowned. "Bring the lamp. Might as well dim the flame."

She carried the lamp to the bedside table and set it down. Noah turned down the wick. The room darkened. His hand found hers. Threading his fingers through hers, he coaxed her to the bed and drew her into his arms.

Her heart thundered against her ribs. An image flashed in her mind. The face of the man on the ship. She tightened her shoulders. Desperation pressed down on her chest. Her breath grew shallow. His arms felt strong and comforting and yet the fear persisted. The feeling of powerlessness. Every part of her wanted to break free, to escape Noah's embrace.

"S'all right." He kissed the back of her head. "Sarah, it's all right, I promise."

Her breathing slowed. She closed her eyes. The dove's soft coo calmed her a little more. Her heartbeat steadied.

"Okay?" he asked.

"Yes."

"You need to rest. Can't have you stumblin' around when it's time to make my cinnamon rolls."

She gave a breathless laugh. Holding her forearm, he stroked her wrist with his thumb. His touch sent a shiver up her spine, but the sensation brought none of the usual dread. She drew a deep shuddering breath and sank deeper into the shelter of his arms. Tucking her close, he sighed contentedly.

"I didn't intend to make cinnamon rolls," she whispered.

He growled softly.

She smiled. "I just made cinnamon rolls yesterday."

He replied with an indistinct grumble. "I didn't get a single one," he muttered.

"Cinnamon rolls?"

"The boys devoured the whole basket. Took 'em all of two minutes. I turned my back to hunt for the salt and pepper for my eggs and come back to find a table of boys wearing guilty expressions."

Sarah recalled the way the boys' faces lit with joy when she came to the table with a pan of hot rolls. They'd chattered with excitement as she set the rolls in the basket. It took so little to bring smiles to their faces. The memory made her eyes water with a surge of deep affection.

Anytime she could make their lives a little brighter, it served to illuminate her heart with a bright abiding light. It was simple. The children made her happy. They had from the beginning, she realized as she lay in Noah's arms. To her surprise, she felt the same about Noah. If she could please him with something as simple as baking cinnamon rolls then she yearned to do just that.

While she hadn't planned on baking rolls for breakfast, she had two pans of bread on the counter, proofing for dinner. It was a simple solution. She could use the bread dough for breakfast and still have time to make more for dinner.

"All right, Mr. Bailey," she said softly. "I'll bake you whatever your heart desires."

Waiting for a response, she realized he'd fallen asleep. His breathing was deep and even. His arms were comforting and even though he slept, his hold on her was firm.

Chapter Twenty-Seven

Noah

The feed room could use a good cleaning and maybe a coat of paint. Noah eyed the bins, noting the rust on the latches. He ought to have the boys replace the hardware. Lately Holden took on more jobs and did them so well that Noah hardly had to check his work.

The boy even managed to organize the rest of the boys. Not only that, he kept the peace too. A remarkable accomplishment considering how much they'd squabbled in the beginning. There'd been a few fights along the way, nothing terrible, just a few fat lips. It was all over soon enough. Just the same, Noah was glad the boys didn't resort to fighting too often.

He leaned back in the chair and strummed the guitar. He'd found the instrument tucked in a trunk along with a few other things from his youth. He'd taken the trunk to the new house and sorted the contents. When he found the guitar, he formed a plan.

If Sarah wasn't going to tell him what was going on with Holden, he'd ask the boy himself. All he needed was a little something to sweeten the deal. A guitar would help loosen the boy's tongue.

A few moments later, the feed room door opened. Walt stuck his head in. "I found him for you, sir."

"Thank you, son. Let us be, would you?"

Holden pushed him out of the way and came in, a somber expression on his face. When he spied the guitar, he relaxed his shoulders a notch. He still looked fretful, probably wondering if he was in trouble. Walt shut the door and trotted out of the barn.

"Everything all right?" Holden asked.

Noah grimaced at the boy's tone. The first time he'd had a talk with Holden, the boy had been certain he was in for a whipping. Noah only wanted to show him how to mend a pair of reins. He'd hated to see the fear in Holden's eyes and never wanted the boy to worry.

"It's fine. I just wanted to chat a moment, that's all. Have a seat. What do you think of my guitar?"

"It's real nice," Holden said, his tone cordial.

Noah hit a note wrong deliberately and noted the pained look on Holden's eyes. He smiled inwardly. The boy had an ear for music. That's what Pastor James said. Even the Sweet Willow teacher praised his talent and that was saying something. She and Holden hadn't been on good terms from what the other boys said.

"I just bet you could teach yourself to play this guitar," Noah mused.

Holden gave him a tentative smile, sensing that the guitar would come at a price. "Maybe."

He tried for an indifferent tone, holding out to see what Noah was getting at. In the past they'd argued about school and whether Holden would go in the fall. Noah told him he needed to attend. Holden maintained he was a grown-up and school was for babies.

"If you don't want it, I could ask the other boys," Noah suggested. "Josiah might like a guitar."

Holden twitched. For a long moment, Noah watched as the boy's yearning for the instrument warred with his pride. The desire won out. "I suppose I'd like to try to play."

Noah made no move to give him the guitar. Instead, he continued plucking the strings, not in a particularly melodious way. Holden, unable to fully mask his emotions, winced a few times.

"I got to wondering. You've been helping Sarah in the evenings for close to a week now. That right?"

A wary look passed behind Holden's eyes. He nodded slowly. "Yessir."

"It concerned me a tad, especially the first couple of evenings. You looked a little riled up."

Holden jerked to his feet. "Did she tell you something?"

"Not a thing. But if there's some trouble between you and Sarah, I'd like to know."

The boy ran his fingers through his hair and settled back in the chair, looking even more uncomfortable than before.

Noah set the guitar aside. He leaned forward, setting his elbows on his knees. "I know it's not easy having a lady come live in the house. Probably seems strange at times. Just the same, I reckon it's pretty nice to have her here. Sorta surprised how much I like it, truth be told."

Holden knit his brows. "Course it is. Sarah's real nice to all of us."

"So what's she got you doing that made you mad?"

"She..." The boy's words drifted off. He licked his lips then pressed them together.

"Is this a difficult question? I expected you to say something about washing dishes."

"She asks me to read her stories. Stories that she writes. I read them and tell her what I think."

Noah narrowed his eyes and kept his gaze fixed on Holden, waiting for the boy to show a sign that he was making up tales. Not that the boy fibbed. Ever. Still, Noah could hardly believe what he was hearing.

"It's true," Holden insisted. "She wrote a story about a boy who is hunting down a couple of outlaws. It's just him and his dog, riding through the desert, trying to bring the desperados to justice. He doesn't even have a gun or anything. The bad guys had him for a while, but Landon got away. They had him tied up with his own twine. After they fell asleep, he cut the twine with a cactus needle."

Noah's jaw dropped. "Cactus needles?"

Holden scoffed. "I didn't think that was very good. I sorta wondered if she'd ever looked close at a cactus needle."

Both Noah and Holden chuckled.

"Probably not," Noah said.

"She thinks they're sharp on the sides along with being pointy. Like a knife or something."

They laughed at the notion of cactus knives.

"Then she wrote about a farmer milking a steer, and he made butter from the steer milk."

"I don't believe it."

"The bad guys rode all the way from Houston to El Paso."

"Come on now."

"Then they turned right around and rode back, making both trips in half an hour. She's got a lady pony express rider named Millicent."

"Millicent?"

Holden nodded. "And she smokes cigars."

By then Holden's eyes had begun to water. He held his stomach as he laughed and Noah laughed right along with him, shaking his head with disbelief.

Noah got to his feet and offered the guitar to Holden. "Didn't expect to hear all this, but I'm glad."

Holden sobered. "Yes, sir. So am I. Sarah's nice, every bit as nice as Aunt Laura." They left the feed room and walked through the barn.

He went on. "I wish I could do something nice for her."

"Like what?"

"Like get her a good stove for the new house."

"What's that supposed to mean? Good stove?"

Holden gave a triumphant smile, pleased that he knew something about Sarah that Noah didn't. "It's too small. It just has two burners and it takes a lot longer to cook some meals. The oven's not big enough."

The boy gave him a knowing smile. The self-assuredness rankled Noah. He didn't particularly care to learn news about his wife from his son. Holden was plenty smart, to be sure, but it wasn't right that he knew about Sarah's preferences before Noah.

How did Holden know Sarah needed a bigger oven? This was why he wanted to share a bedroom with Sarah, just like every other man and wife. He wanted her company. He yearned to be near her. If they spent evenings together, they'd talk of things she needed and then he could make sure she had just what she wanted.

"I'll take good care of your guitar, sir," Holden said as they walked to the house.

Noah's irritation faded. The way Holden smiled appreciatively and the way he wore an expression of pure gratitude warmed Noah's heart. He wished that he'd given the guitar to Holden in the beginning. He had no doubt the boy would soon play much better than Noah ever could.

"I'm sure you will, son." Noah tousled the boy's hair. "Especially since it's your guitar now."

Chapter Twenty-Eight

Sarah

When Sarah went to the new house, it was the first time she'd been inside by herself. She'd visited with Noah, of course, and tidied the sawdust and shavings with the boys. She'd met with the carpenter when he had questions about wood trim on the stairs. Never alone, however.

Her footfalls echoed in the empty hallway. Stopping in the doorway of the dining room, she studied the oak table that Noah had built for the family. It was more than twice the size of the table they used now. Tracing her fingers along the decorative edge, Sarah couldn't decide what she thought of the new table. It was lovely, yes. But the other table, with its mismatched chairs and cramped space, made for a close, intimate feel. She would miss sitting around the crowded table.

And yet, the extra space might offer room for more children. A flurry of emotions circled her chest. More children. Was that what Noah wanted? Without a moment's consideration, she knew the answer was yes. She tried to picture him with a baby in his arms.

Laura came to the front door, interrupting her thoughts. Dustin and Josiah each carried a basket filled with linens. They trailed behind Laura; their faces wreathed in smiles. Laura smiled too but she was pale and, after the boys left, complained of having morning sickness earlier that day.

"It's a good sign," Laura said, sounding cheerful as she unpacked the curtains from the basket.

Sarah took a swath of linen and unfolded it, laying it across the dining table. The fabric was gauzy, delicate and trimmed with exquisite lace. Sarah could hardly tear her gaze from the pretty curtains.

"Do you like them?" Laura asked.

"So beautiful. I've never seen such lovely curtains."

"Will Noah mind lace curtains in his room?" Laura gave her a mischievous smile. "It might come as a bit of a shock to the man."

Sarah blushed. Her face warmed and she laughed nervously. "Yes, well, we haven't discussed the curtains or anything about the room, really. I think he intends to leave the details up to me."

Laura nodded, the impish smile still playing upon her lips.

"I worry about that," Sarah said. "You know?"

She prayed that Laura would get her meaning and wouldn't make her explain.

"It will be fine, Sarah. You two suit each other. I'm certain God intended for the two of you to meet and marry. Noah is a fine man and he's lucky to have you."

"I still haven't told him."

Laura held up a curtain to examine the hem. She lowered it to give Sarah a questioning look. "Told him what?"

"That the main reason I came to Texas was to find my sister. I'm afraid he'll be angry. Or that I'll disappoint him."

Laura shrugged. "Well, he'll just have to get happy in the same little boots he got mad in."

Sarah let out a sharp breath, that was part laughter, part gasp. Laura's eyes twinkled. "I can't wait till you meet Eleanor, Caleb's aunt. She's full of sayings like that. I'm sure she wouldn't be afraid of her marriage bed. Her husband might be a tad nervous, but not Eleanor."

Laura went upstairs to the bedroom with Sarah following behind. They worked in the bedroom, hanging the curtains, while they talked more.

Laura tried to set her mind at ease. "Every bride has butterflies. It's natural."

"I suppose I'll tell him about Abigail when we move in. I need a couple more days to build up my courage."

Laura eyed the bedroom door. It hadn't been hung yet but leaned against the wall. "As soon as the doors are hung, I believe Noah intends to have the boys begin moving things to the house. The carpenter has a lot of the new furniture in the barn. It won't be long now."

"I know," Sarah said softly, her stomach swirling again.

Chapter Twenty-Nine

Josiah

Thunder rumbled, shaking the small house. All morning, he and the other boys moved things to the new house. Josiah wished they could finish, but they couldn't be out in the rain. Noah didn't want stuff getting wet, which meant they probably couldn't sleep in their new house that night.

He felt antsy. And mighty disappointed. If only the darned rain could have stayed away for a few more days.

He wandered into the kitchen where Sarah stood peeling potatoes. She wore a pretty, yellow dress, her hair a little mussed like it often was when she worked in the kitchen. She blew at her hair, trying to get it out of her eyes, but the curl just bounced a little and went right back to the same spot.

"Hello, Josiah. I thought you might be up at the new house."

"No, ma'am. The others are up there working on a gutter on the back porch."

"But not you?"

He'd wanted to help, but he'd accidentally bumped Holden's ladder and got fussed at by the older boy. Holden told him he was too little to help. He was a nuisance and should go find something else to do. Josiah had his feelings hurt and came home.

He shook his head. She gave him a look, her eyes sort of big and her mouth tugged down a notch. Like she felt sorry for him. Which made his eyes sting. Every time.

"I wanted to help you," he replied, which was not exactly a lie, but not exactly the truth either.

She dropped the potato into a pot of water. It plopped, sloshing a bit of water over the edge. With a swipe of a cloth, she dried the spill. "I'm so glad you're here. I need help from someone brave."

"I'm brave." He frowned. Somehow the words jumped out of his mouth. He hadn't even taken a moment to consider what she might really be asking.

She dried her hands on her apron, untied the ribbons and set it on the counter. "Ever since Walt told me about snakes that eat eggs, I've been afraid of venturing into the chicken coop by myself."

"I can help you. I'm not afraid of snakes."

"Thank goodness." She took a basket from the shelf and they left the house. Walking side by side, they made the short trip to the coop.

"Snakes like to move around when a storm's coming." Josiah glanced up at the darkening sky. "I wonder how they know."

When Sarah didn't reply, he turned to find her eyeing him. "Ma'am?"

"Sometimes I think you boys tell tales just to alarm me. When Holden talked about the snake that likes eggs, I didn't believe him."

"You didn't?"

"Not a word. I wanted to ask him if the snakes prefer their eggs fried or scrambled."

Josiah chuckled. "Snakes like eggs any way they can get em."

He opened the door of the coop for her and waited for her to go in first. Noah had told the boys different things men are supposed to do for ladies and opening doors was one of them. Sarah didn't seem to want to go in. She just stood there like her feet were rooted to the spot.

"Is it safe to go in?" she asked.

"Safe from what?"

She sighed. "From snakes."

"Sure it is. I can go in first if you like."

He wasn't certain if Noah would consider it bad manners if he went in first but the look in her eyes had made him speak without thinking. Again.

She nodded. "I would like that. Thank you, Josiah."

Stepping inside the coop, he made a show of looking around even though he was pretty sure there weren't any snakes. For one, he hadn't ever seen one. For two, Lucy, the gray tabby cat lazed on the top roost, her tail hanging out. She gave a sleepy yawn and trilled.

Most of the chickens were in the yard, pecking and scratching. Only one remained, dozing in her box.

"No snakes. Lucy keeps an eye out for snakes. She's in here."

Sarah smiled as she stepped inside the coop and together, they gathered the eggs. They chatted about the different colored eggs and the chickens. She told him about growing up in a big city and how she'd never stepped foot in a chicken coop. She'd never been around animals either but she liked all of them.

"Except the snakes," she added.

199

"Nobody likes snakes," Josiah assured her. "Not even other snakes. Take for example the king snake. They eat rattlesnakes."

Sarah gave him a disbelieving look and sighed. They passed the cat as they left the coop. Lucy gave another trill, flicked her tail and rolled onto her back. Sarah reached up to pet the cat.

Josiah stopped her. "She'll swat you when she's feeling playful like that."

"How do you know she's feeling playful?"

"She's on her back. Her eyes look sorta wild."

Sarah's brows lifted. She looked impressed. Josiah pushed his shoulders back a notch. Finally, someone who didn't think everything he said was dumb or wrong. He nodded solemnly. "It's best to avoid upside down cats."

She pursed her lips. "Thank you kindly, Josiah. I do appreciate your help and your excellent judgment."

They returned to the small house, talking about puddles and wet grass. Their pace was unhurried. They paused to watch a hawk soar across the stormy sky. Partway home, Sarah asked him to tell her more about snakes and cats and whatnot. A light mist fell. Thunder rumbled, but Josiah no longer minded if it poured.

Chapter Thirty

Sarah

The first day in the new house, Sarah worked from dawn until past dark. There was so much to do and so much to think about. Noah and the boys worked in the auction barn, busy with a sheep and goat sale. Laura offered to come help, but Sarah wouldn't think of it. She didn't want Laura to work in her home when she had her own duties to attend.

Despite Sarah's refusal, Laura sent dinner for the family. A good thing too. Sarah's kitchen didn't have a stove. Not yet. She needed to speak to Noah about bringing the stove from the other house in the next few days.

The boys were excited about their new rooms, but tired from the day. After their baths, they trudged off to bed and soon were fast asleep.

Sarah came upstairs to get ready for bed. She'd waited a long time to confess, or so it seemed to her. Now the time had come and with each passing moment, she grew more fretful.

A box lay on the bed. When she opened it, she found a note from Laura.

I know you regretted not saying your vows in church and hoped to do so one day. I took the liberty of making a dress for you. I hope and pray that you'll like it and wear it one day soon. I know you'll look beautiful.

Sarah felt a sob well up in her throat. Tracing her fingers over the tissue, she couldn't find the will to look at the dress. Anything Laura made would be beautiful, of course. But Sarah might never wear it, not if Noah rejected her apology. Even if he forgave her, he'd likely consider saying vows in church wasn't necessary. He was a practical man. A busy man. How could she convince her gruff husband that a church wedding could be a blessing?

When Noah came into their room, he said a few words of greeting. He changed out of his work clothes and washed up. A few moments later, he came to her chair, stopping behind her. She sat at a dressing table with a mirror. He studied her reflection.

"You're ready for bed," he said gently, eyeing her gown. "Unless..."

A smile tugged at his lips as he ran his finger over a pin tucked in her hair.

"Unless?" she asked softly.

"Unless you wear your hair like this when you sleep. Is this how ladies sleep? With a bunch of hair pins stuck in their hair?"

If she hadn't been so nervous, she might have smiled at his teasing.

"I always take it down. Sometimes I braid it. Like I did when you came to my room the other day."

Neither of them had spoken of the night he'd strolled into her room and stretched out on her bed. They certainly hadn't talked of how she lay in his arms just as the sun peeked over the horizon. At some point, as the new day dawned, they'd come to an unspoken agreement that their union was no longer a marriage of convenience.

Which had brought them to this point. Their first night together as man and wife. She had to tell him everything, even if the prospect filled her with dread. She couldn't bear the notion of disappointing Noah.

He didn't say a word about the other night. Instead, he tugged the pin free, set it on the nearby table and proceeded to pull each pin from her hair. Swathes of her blonde hair tumbled past her shoulders. When he removed the last hairpin, he set his hands on the back of her chair.

"You want to tell me something." He stated the words as if he already knew she meant to speak about a troubling topic. "I want to tell you something too."

Alarm trickled down her spine. The memory of the Beckers' home in San Francisco came rushing back. She'd grown up thinking she belonged there. In the space of a single heartbeat, the home belonged to someone else. In the days after losing Erna and Otto, she found that she'd lost her home too.

The memory sent a shard of pain through her heart. She shivered. Her hands felt clammy even though she felt a chill.

He frowned. "How about I go first?"

"Yes," she whispered. "Please."

He gave her a lopsided smile. "Apparently, you said a few words to Holden about your stove."

"What?"

"You told him it's a little small for our big family. You have to cook in batches which takes a long time."

"Did he think I was complaining?"

"No. Not one bit. But he was complaining on your behalf. Sorta surprising. He said I should get you a bigger stove. I ordered one from Houston and it will be here tomorrow at noon."

"My goodness."

"I bought the finest one they had. I would have taken you there to pick it out, but I wanted to surprise you."

She sat motionless, trying to think of what to say.

"Now, Sarah." He took the brush from the table and began to brush her hair. "It's your turn. Tell me what's troubling you."

She nodded, fidgeted with her hands as she summoned her courage. She gave a small murmur of frustration and snatched his letter from the table. He stopped brushing her hair, gazed at the letter and returned his attention to her hair and the brush.

"You kept my letter," he remarked.

"You did not write that letter." Her voice sounded accusatory, sharp and almost shrill.

"I confess I did not write the entire letter. What about it?"

She cast the letter aside. "After my parents passed away, I found letters about a sister I had. In Boston. I traveled to Boston and discovered that her name was Abigail Winthrop. She had traveled to Texas to marry Caleb Walker."

Her heart raced. She hadn't intended to blurt the words. Once she started, the confession poured out in a wild rush as if it had gotten tired of waiting.

Noah's jaw dropped and he stared at her with disbelief. "I'll be."

"I agreed to your proposal so I could meet my sister."

Staring at her, he nodded thoughtfully. "Of course. You favor her. The eyes. The smile." After studying her for a long moment, his lips curved into a grin. "That's your secret? Abigail Walker is your sister."

"Yes," she said, feeling a little sheepish.

He chuckled, set the brush aside and drew her from the chair. "So, I don't need to worry about fighting off a bunch of fellas?"

"Noah. How can you tease me at a time like this?"

His smile widened and amusement glinted in his eyes.

"You're a heartless... beast."

"That's too bad for you, since you're stuck with this heartless beast. And this heartless beast can't wait to introduce his pretty bride to her newfound sister."

He stopped beside the bed, his smile fading as he took her hands in his. "Sarah," he said gently, his eyes lit with a soft light. "You could have told me about your sister. It's my fault you didn't have the confidence to tell me. At first, I only wanted to do right by the boys. I didn't think about being a good husband to you."

He lifted her hands and kissed the back of each wrist. "I didn't know you. But now I do, and you know me. God put us together for a reason. We're meant to be man and wife."

She drew a trembling breath.

He nodded at the bed. "I heard a rumor. About a wedding dress."

"It's true. Laura made it for me."

Wincing, Noah let out a low groan. "Another wedding?"

She nodded. "Maybe when Abigail returns to Sweet Willow."

He kept on, feigning deep annoyance. "More wedding business. Which means I need to corral the boys, order them into their church clothes. Make Dustin comb his hair."

"We could even have a wedding cake."

"Well, then." His brows lifted. "That changes everything."

"I've never made a wedding cake before."

He wandered to the bed and reached for the box. Sarah darted to his side and swatted his hand away. The gesture drew a chuckle from him.

"You can't see the dress, Noah. It's considered bad luck."

"All right. Let's have this shindig as soon as Abigail comes back."

"We can talk to the Pastor James when we go to church on Sunday. He might not be able to conduct the ceremony right away."

"That's all right. It gives us a little time to plan something special. In the meantime, I'd like to mention we've been married almost a month." He offered a slow, sultry smile and bent to whisper. "I have to confess that I'm an eager groom."

Her face warmed but she didn't offer a word of protest. Instead, she looped her arm around his neck and let him pull her into his embrace.

He lowered to brush a kiss across her lips, a sweet, loving kiss that filled her heart with a rush of warmth. Trailing a line of kisses to her ear, he whispered. "We will never need to keep any secrets. I'm yours. You're mine."

Chapter Thirty-One

Noah

A knock at the door pulled Noah from his dreams. He grumbled. Ever since the boys came to live with him, he'd paid close attention to any sound. Ever since Sarah had come, they hadn't suffered any nightmares. Before Sarah, he was used to getting up to check on the boys. Not anymore.

It had been two weeks since moving to the new house, two weeks of sharing a room with Sarah. He relished the feel of his wife as she slept next to him. As he dozed, he was vaguely aware that resting next to his wife made waking in the middle of the night a considerable chore. There wasn't anything he liked more than the way Sarah nestled close to him at night. She felt warm. She smelled like sweet sugary flowers.

Maybe he'd only imagined the sound of someone knocking. Daybreak would come soon enough. He tucked Sarah closer into his embrace. He kissed the top of her head. It was probably getting to be time to get up, but he wanted to linger.

She stirred. "Did I hear a boy at the door?" she whispered.

Another knock sounded. This time a little louder.

"There's your answer," he said, his voice rough from sleep.

She sat up. He put his hand on her shoulder to keep her from leaving the warm bed. "I'll take care of it."

Opening the door, Noah found Holden standing at the threshold with a lamp. The flame flickered. His expression was solemn, his eyes wide. Noah was instantly wide awake.

"What's the matter?"

"A fella came to speak to you. He works for the Rangers. With Beau. They're riding the territory around the mines, looking for the Montgomery brothers. One of Beau's men got shot. He's sent for help, but the nearest Rangers are in the valley, at least three days' ride."

Noah was instantly awake. "I didn't hear anyone come by. I'm glad you did."

"I was up early. Are you going to go help? Can I come?"

"The answers are yes and no. In that order. Go saddle the big roan gelding."

"Yessir." Holden did a poor job of concealing his disappointment. He sighed and turned back to his room to put on his work clothes and boots.

Noah closed the door and began dressing in the predawn darkness. Sarah got up and put on a robe. He sensed her dismay. He hated to leave her and the boys, but the threat of the Montgomery brothers had returned to Sweet Willow.

Just last week, the men had tried to lure two youngsters away from home. They promised riches working in the mines. Noah had begun to suspect some of the boys' nightmares had come from seeing the men lurking around Sweet Willow.

If Beau was about to collar the men, Noah intended to make sure his cousin had a man by his side. If his deputy was injured, that man would be Noah.

He'd ridden with Beau in the past, but he hadn't been a family man in those days. He didn't want to leave. Not today. Not ever. But it couldn't be helped.

Just last night he and Sarah spoke about her meeting Abigail. She fretted, wondering if her sister would welcome her. Maybe Abigail would resent her and the parents who hadn't returned for her. Noah was certain that would not be so.

The meeting was one of a thousand reasons he didn't want to leave. Abigail and Caleb were expected back any day now. Noah would have liked to be with his wife when the two sisters finally met.

Sarah lit the lamp on her bedside table.

"No need to get up, Sarah." He made a point of keeping his tone light. He wasn't sure how much she'd heard about the circumstances.

"I could make you coffee." She crossed the room, stopping a few paces from him. "A quick bite to eat."

"I'd rather be on my way."

The soft light of the lamp lit her features, tight with worry. He dressed hurriedly. Regret twisted inside him. If only he'd taken care of things when he'd first come face to face with the men at the train station. If he'd done the right thing, he would have stopped their evil trade. He hadn't though. And now a man was shot. Noah grimaced. Self-recrimination weighed heavily on his shoulders.

"For how long?" she asked quietly.

"More than likely just a few days." He pulled on his boots and took his hat from the hook.

She nodded. "All right, Noah."

Grateful that she didn't fuss or argue, he offered a smile. He took her into his arms and pulled her close, relishing the way she melted into his embrace. She laid her cheek against his chest. He hated to leave her, especially like this. Especially now. They'd started a new life together. At night, they'd talk about things to come and frequently spoke about the prospect of their own children. Sarah could be in the family way already.

They stood in silence for a long moment until he forced himself to step away.

"I'll be back as soon as I can. Maybe Abigail will be home by then. We'll have that church wedding."

"That sounds wonderful."

"I'd rather you keep this to yourself." He stopped at the door, his hand on the knob. "Holden knows, of course, but I'd rather you not discuss matters with the younger boys."

"Of course." Her eyes shone in the lamp light, but she didn't shed a tear. For that he was grateful. He nodded and left. Downstairs, he strapped on his gun and belt, took the Winchester from the cabinet and left the house.

Holden waited outside, holding the reins of the roan gelding that Noah favored.

"I'm leaving you in charge, Holden." He put the rifle in the scabbard and took the reins. "While I'm gone, you're the man of the house."

"You can depend on me, sir." His voice faltered, but his expression was resolute.

"Don't talk to the other boys about this. No need for them to worry."

"Yessir."

"If I haven't gotten back in two days' time, I want you to ask your Uncle Seth to come run the cattle sale. He'll know what to do. If not, you tell him how we do things. Clear?"

"Yessir."

Noah swung into the saddle, bid the boy farewell and set off into the predawn darkness.

Chapter Thirty-Two

Sarah

With Noah gone, nothing seemed the same. Even the weather had shifted that afternoon, and as night fell the temperature dropped, heralding an ominous storm. Sarah stirred the gravy and prepared to serve dinner. A blast of thunder boomed overhead, shaking the house.

She set the spoon down and leaned out the kitchen door. Holden sat on a chair by the fire. The boys sat cross-legged on the rug listening to him read the story of Landon's adventures. The boys had squabbled all day, particularly Dustin and Josiah and now they sat quietly. Sarah felt a wave of appreciation for Holden.

When Sarah wrote the story for him, she'd intended to create a story that Holden would want to read. One that was easy but not too simple, one that held his attention. That was Sarah's only aim. She'd read plenty of Westerns to Otto and found the storytelling easy enough. When she'd first put pen to paper, she couldn't have imagined her husband heading out into the wilds to pursue two outlaws like the boy in the story.

She wasn't sure if the boys noted the parallel, but they did like to hear the story. This was the third or fourth time Holden had read to the boys. Sarah noted the ease with which he read. He'd improved so much in a short time. The boy had a fine mind, indeed.

She smiled at the group. None of them seemed at all concerned about the storm that had descended upon them. Even though they'd heard the story before, they were far too involved in Landon's bravado to pay the storm any mind.

Holden met her gaze, setting aside the worn pages of the story. He looked concerned, maybe because she did as well.

"That was some loud thunder, for sure," he said.

Sarah smiled inwardly, recalling Noah's comments about Holden pointing out obvious facts. Her worry eased a little. She let out a breath and let her shoulders relax to some small degree.

"Loud indeed," Sarah replied. She took a cowboy hat from a nearby table and set it on her head. It was too large by far, probably belonging to Noah. The rim covered her eyes. She tipped it back and tried to lower her tone a few notches. "Why, I 'bout jumped clear outta my boots."

The boys grinned at her attempt to mimic Noah. With the tip of her forefinger, she tilted her hat back a little more. "If you boys are ready to eat a bite," she said, keeping her voice low, "I reckon you'd best wash yer hands. Clear?"

This version of Noah was too much. The boys laughed and added their own impression of the man. They ambled off to the washroom as a group. They swaggered, grumbled and drew their brows into a heavy frown as they growled orders at each other. Even Holden joined in the game of poking fun at Noah in his absence.

"All right. No dawdling," he barked, drawing another round of laughter from the boys.

Sarah waited by the stove, ready to serve the boys when they lined up. In her heart, she felt certain to keep to the routine. They'd share a nice meal together and after they'd enjoy a slice of chocolate cake. Everything would be ordinary, that was her firm intention.

The boys' joking gave way to bickering as Josiah and Dustin argued. Holden tried to intervene which helped until the boys lined up in the kitchen. Dustin and Josiah jostled each other and muttered a few insults under their breath.

Sarah assumed they'd settle down as she served each boy. To her dismay, the boys' voices grew louder. Walt joined in and soon Hugo offered a harsh reply, telling all of them to quit acting like babies. This made Dustin sneer at Josiah and call him a baby.

This was too much for Josiah. He lunged at Dustin. Fists flew, one hit Hugo squarely on the jaw. He responded with a loud, obscene word which drew a shout of dismay from Holden. Josiah managed to land a few blows, sending Dustin to the floor. Josiah pounced screaming. In the next instant, Josiah was under Dustin. Holden commanded them to stop. The boys ignored him.

Sarah watched in a daze at the astonishing scene unfolding in the kitchen. Josiah's wail of pain yanked her from her confusion. With three quick steps, she darted to where Dustin pummeled Josiah. She grabbed the bigger boy's shoulder, imploring him to stop.

There was a blur. And a burst of pain and flash of light. One moment Sarah had been on her feet. The next, she sat on her bottom in a very unladylike posture.

The fighting ceased. The boys stared. The kitchen filled with silence.

"Oh," Sarah said with surprise. "Something hit my eye."

A murmur of dismay moved over the boys. They gaped at her transfixed as if she'd sprouted another head. She blinked several times. Her eye watered, tears dripped down. Slowly she lifted her hand to her eye.

All six boys shouted at the same time. *No! Don't touch it. Stop. Dang, that's bad, so bad.*

"What happened?" Sarah asked.

Holden crouched by her side. "You got hit. Want me to help you up?"

Sarah laughed softly. "Well, I can't sit here, can I?"

Holden took one arm, Walt the other, and they helped Sarah to her feet. They waited a moment before letting go. She shooed them away, wanting nothing more than to forget about the incident. She served the boys and spoke lightly of the matter. It was an accident. Nothing more. It didn't even hurt.

Dustin, however, grew more distressed. He refused his dinner, sat at the table looking distraught and fought to keep from crying. He muttered a few words about the fight and seemed certain it was his elbow that struck Sarah. Josiah ate dinner, but hardly looked up from his plate. Holden hardly spoke and seemed to think the fight was his fault for not keeping the peace.

After the meal, Holden insisted she rest while the boys tidied the kitchen. The boys all followed his directions quietly. There wasn't any further rancor. Later, they bid her goodnight and went to their rooms. When she went into the kitchen, she found it spotless. The chocolate cake sat on the counter, untouched.

The storm continued through the evening. Sarah glanced in the living room mirror several times to see the astonishing changes to her injury. Her eye swelled so much she could scarcely open it. The boys regarded her with astonishment and dismay. Holden, looking glum, suggested her eye would look worse in the morning, swollen, dark, perhaps even black.

Each boy came to bid her good night.

She went to her room, her heart heavy. The bruised eye didn't trouble her. Not as much as Dustin's distress. There was a time when she'd been vain. It troubled her to think on that. But that time had passed. Now she was more troubled by a boy's hurting heart than a bruise.

Even the prospect of meeting Abigail didn't linger in her mind that evening. She wished for peace in the home. Harmony. She wanted her husband to return. With him gone, their home seemed empty.

Heading upstairs, she wondered how she could sleep without him. When she entered the room, she crossed to his side of the bed. Tracing her fingers over his pillow, she tried to imagine where he was.

"Noah, come home," she whispered. "Please, come home."

She moved to the window and watched the storm play out along the distant horizon. The sight made her fret. Her unease notched up, but eased somewhat when she said a prayer for his safe return.

Just before she undressed and got ready for bed, she took a lamp in hand and went to the boys' rooms. She peeked in the room where Holden and his brothers slept. All three rested quietly. She listened to the deep breathing and smiled at the memory of Holden's efforts to fill Noah's shoes. All day, he'd tried to corral the boys and keep order. He'd viewed the fight in the kitchen, and especially her injury, as a personal failing. In the morning, she'd be sure to make light of everything. Next, she went to the room where Josiah, Walt and Dustin slept. She lifted the lamp. Josiah dozed, as did Walt.

Dustin was not in his bed.

The boy was gone.

Chapter Thirty-Three

Noah

The narrow path they called Sendero Ridge skirted the Sierra Mountains. Beau and Noah rode single file, never a good idea when there was a threat of ambush. Every so often the horses loosened rocks and pebbles as they picked their way along the trail. The stones tumbled down the steep face of the mountain, picking up other rocks along the way.

The rockfall sent an echo along the canyon.

Beau rode ahead. Each time the stones fell, he shook his head. Noah grimaced. He didn't like it any better. It couldn't be helped.

The trail widened. Beau halted his horse to give Noah's horse a chance to catch up. They let both horses take a well-deserved rest. Sweat covered their necks, chests and flanks. The ride up the mountain had taxed both animals.

Beau reached for his canteen. Noah's throat was parched, but he hardly noticed. He was more interested in the outcropping a dozen paces ahead. He gestured to the mountain's craggy feature. Beau froze.

Noah slipped from the saddle, handed the reins to Beau and unholstering his gun, moved toward the rocky outcrop. Cautiously, he leaned around the rocks. He found a gap, a narrow opening that led to a cave. Peering inside, he found it empty.

He was about to tell Beau there was nothing to see when in fact a flash of movement drew his eyes. Holding up his hand, he pressed against the rock wall. Two horses grazed some distance down the path. When one shifted, it became clear that they wore full tack. But why?

Could it be a trap? Noah watched a moment longer. The other horse took a step and, while Noah couldn't see perfectly, it was clear the animal had snagged its reins. Even at some distance, Noah could tell the horse had caught himself. It jerked back, almost rearing with a panicked retreat.

From that, Noah could tell that something had happened to the Montgomery brothers. They'd left their horses unattended. It likely was not a trap, but he couldn't be sure. Not only had one horse snapped its reins, the men risked their horses running off without them.

Noah holstered his gun and returned to Beau to explain what he'd seen.

"The heck," Beau muttered. "Did they stop to take a beauty rest?"

"Maybe so. But they ought to have secured their horses a little better before napping."

Beau shook his head as he offered a wry grin.

"Might be a trap but my gut says no." Noah took a drink from his canteen before mounting his horse.

"I'm inclined to agree."

They rode down the path. Their horses pricked their ears at the sight of the other animals and gave low whickers. The Montgomery mounts, a pair of flashy palominos, continued grazing.

Noah dismounted first and managed to catch the two palominos. Both horses had fine saddles and bridles made of dark leather and trimmed in silver. Noah hadn't ever seen anything so fancy and fought a wave of anger. The men had bought and paid for the tack by abusing young kids.

Both horses showed signs of poor treatment, which wasn't much of a surprise, considering. The animals had been spurred and whipped. Both were skittish. Noah tamped down his temper. Now was not the time to get angry. Now was the time to make sure it didn't happen again.

Noah and Beau secured the horses. They moved slowly to the edge of the cliff and looked over.

On a ledge below lay the crumpled body of one of the men. The man didn't move. A few paces away lay the other Montgomery brother who was still alive but in a bad way.

Noah and Beau made their way down the steep embankment. Neither drew their weapons. It was clear that the Montgomery brothers were no threat.

When Noah knelt beside Sal, he saw that the man wasn't long for this world. He rasped a few words about his brother. Noah shook his head.

Sal spoke again. "Don't leave us here."

Beau scoffed at Sal's words. He muttered a remark about what the men deserved. His cousin held a grudge about his injured deputy. Noah held bad feelings too. When he'd made the long, hard trip to the Sierra Mountains, he'd imagined this moment. He'd been certain that justice would give him satisfaction.

"Don't leave us," Sal gasped.

"Your brother's dead," Beau spat.

"His horse pitched him. I tried to help." He wheezed, fixing his fading gaze on Noah. "Please, give him a..."

The man's words faded. He closed his eyes, grimacing with pain. Noah waited, watching and wondering if this might be the end for Sal Montgomery. The man's chest rose and fell. He groaned and opened his eyes.

"What do you want me to give him?" Noah asked.

"A Christian burial..."

Chapter Thirty-Four

Sarah

With her lantern in hand, Sarah crept through the house, searching for Dustin. After she made certain he wasn't upstairs, she searched downstairs. Perhaps he'd decided to have a slice of cake. The possibility seemed unlikely. Still, it gave her a desperate surge of hope and she headed first to the kitchen.

The kitchen was empty. The cake sat on the counter undisturbed. She checked the other rooms, starting with Noah's study. Next, the parlor. Finally, the front room where the boys often gathered by the fireplace. He was nowhere to be found.

The door, however, looked to be ajar. Her heart beat a frantic rhythm. She said a silent prayer that her eyes played tricks on her. She'd checked the door before going upstairs. Surely, she'd forgotten to latch the door. That had to be the explanation. Moving slowly to the door, she came to the stark realization that the door was open.

She hurried to the corner room where the boys kept their boots, coats and hats. Dustin's boots were missing. His hat was gone too.

Hastily, she donned a pair of shoes and rushed out the door. The rain had stopped, thank goodness. The storm had passed, leaving the ground a sodden, muddy mess. A blessing, she quickly realized when she glimpsed footprints. They led to the barnyard.

Trudging through the mud, she considered what to do with her lantern. If she was going to search the barn, she'd need the light. Noah, however, constantly reminded the boys no lanterns in the barn. One careless moment with a lantern could start a fire, endangering any animals confined to their stalls.

She wrestled with the dilemma. Her progress was hindered by the muddy track. If Dustin had gone to the barn, he had to still be inside, she decided. There was only one set of tracks.

Her heart thudded as she considered the possibility that he might be saddling a horse, intending to leave. Why else would he have trekked out to the barn? She tried to quicken her pace. The question of the lamp in the barn seemed less important. Perhaps Noah would forgive her transgression.

Skirts dragging in the mud, she was slowed by the sloppy path. The distance to the barn seemed longer than usual. The clouds parted, offering light from a halfmoon.

A wave of loneliness came over her as she wondered where Noah could be. He had told her so little before he left, not even when he'd return. His journey might take a few days, or it might take a week.

"If you were here, none of this would have happened," she grumbled, addressing the moon.

The only response came from the squelch of her boots.

"I promise to be very careful with the lamp. I know it's dangerous, but I have to find Dustin."

Talking to herself offered some small comfort. She felt a glimmer of bravery. Yes, the lamp was important, and she couldn't fuss with Noah's rules in the face of an emergency. A missing child was exactly that, she reasoned. She'd go inside the barn, find Dustin with the aid of the lamp and return to the house immediately.

When she found the boy, she'd shake him. Or perhaps hug him. Maybe both. Yes, both.

The thought pleased her, but in that moment, the footing beneath her feet gave way. She stumbled, and fell, landing in the mud. The lamp dropped to the mud and with a faint flicker went dark.

Slowly and with groan of dismay, Sarah regained her feet. She swayed for a moment and let out a deep, weary sigh. "All right, Noah. I suppose you're right about the lamp."

She picked it up and carried it with her the rest of the way to the barn and set it down by the door. Once inside, she called the boy. At first, she spoke softly. Then she raised her voice a notch.

"Dustin! Are you in here?"

Standing in the doorway, she listened intently. The barn was dark as pitch. She'd been inside a time or two but didn't think she could find her way without a light. She'd have to feel her way through the barn.

Her hair drooped down, tickling the side of her face. She brushed it away, and in so doing smeared a muddy path across her cheek. When she tried to wipe her palms on her dress, she only succeeded in making her hands dirtier.

A sound came from the murky depths of the barn. Taking a few tentative steps, she waved her hand in front of her. She thought the aisle led straight into the barn but couldn't recall for certain.

A snuffling sound greeted her ears. She let out a tearful breath. Thank goodness he was here. Dear lord, what if she hadn't discovered him missing? What if he'd managed to saddle a horse and leave under the cover of night? She would never have been able to forgive herself even if Noah had forgiven her.

"Dustin," she said into the darkness, "it's all right. Everything is all right."

She took a few more steps and waited. After what seemed an eternity, another small, mournful sound came from the gloom. Disoriented, Sarah couldn't tell where the sound came from. Her heartbeat thumped heavily. Her breathing quickened.

"I'm not leaving. I won't leave you here. You need to come back to the house where you belong."

Silence.

The darkness unnerved her. The silence weighed heavily, making each breath difficult. Swaying unsteadily, she rubbed her forehead which resulted in more sticky mud distributed across her face.

"I need your help, Dustin. I can't find you in the darkness. I don't know my way." A sob welled in her throat. "Please, Dustin. Let's put this behind us. Tomorrow's a new day. Each morning is a promise that God offers us. If He can forgive us, we can forgive each other. And we can forgive ourselves."

She waited. The only sound came from her shallow breaths. A distant rumble of thunder came from far off, the last remnants of the storm.

"Dustin," she whispered.

"I'm here."

"Oh, child. Thank goodness."

He came to her and hugged her. She wrapped her arms around him in a fierce embrace, as tears fell. They stood quietly for a long moment.

"I was going to leave home." The boy's words were muffled.

"I know."

"I'm afraid of what Noah's gonna say. I don't want him to be mad or disappointed."

"I know. He might not be happy, but that's okay. People can get upset at first. Then they feel better. A family loves each other no matter what."

"My grandpa gave me up. Said I was too much trouble."

His words sent a stab of pain through her heart. She squeezed her eyes shut. Letting out a long, shuddering breath, she kept her firm hold on the boy's narrow shoulders.

"Your grandpa was wrong, Dustin. You're no trouble at all. You're a blessing."

Dustin didn't reply at first. He stayed very still and allowed her to hold him. The darkness no longer seemed so oppressive. The silence seemed peaceful. Her breathing slowed and deepened.

The boy shifted, drawing back slightly. "You're sorta muddy."

"I am completely muddy." She laughed softly and lowered to kiss the top of his head. "I suppose we both are now."

Chapter Thirty-Five

Josiah

Waking the next morning, Josiah leaned over to look at the bunk below, then scanned the other bed. The other boys were already up.

Josiah grumbled under his breath, recalling the previous evening's scuffle in the kitchen. His memory went to the moment Sarah got hurt. He pictured her collapsed on the floor, her hands over her face. If Dustin hadn't been such a turd that wouldn't have happened. He wasn't sure he could ever look at Sarah in the eye again, not after what happened.

Noah might shrug off the boys' fighting, but he'd be mighty displeased to hear about Sarah getting hurt. Noah had talked about the differences between boys and girls, between men and women. Women were to be protected. The subject had come up concerning Francine, not Sarah. Just the same, Josiah knew Noah would have strong words for all the boys, maybe especially for him.

He climbed down the ladder, pausing at the bottom rung to listen. Unfamiliar voices came from Noah and Sarah's room. A couple of ladies were talking. He couldn't make out the words but neither sounded like Sarah.

The smell of bacon floated in the air. His tummy rumbled.

He needed to eat so that he could do his morning chores, but he also wanted to know who was in Noah's room.

Hastily, he dressed and tiptoed down the hallway. To his surprise, Sarah was in bed. He couldn't see her exactly, but he saw the lumpy blankets and spied a tuft of blonde hair. Her hand stuck out from under the blankets. A splotch of mud stuck to her wrist. A pair of her boots lay beside the bed, crusted with more mud.

Why was there mud on her wrist? And her boots? Had she gotten up early to do chores?

He blinked and rubbed his eyes and scanned the room for a sign of Noah. He wasn't there. Maybe he was downstairs. Over by the far window, two ladies sat, talking quietly. One was Aunt Laura. The other Mr. Walker's wife, Miss Abigail. He would have liked to know what they were doing in Sarah's room.

A third voice chimed in. Josiah realized with alarm the voice belonged to Francine. She sat in another chair on the other side of the post. He craned his neck and could catch a glimpse of the top of her head. Her hair was done up in a fussy style. Little Miss High and Mighty wagged her head back and forth as she talked. Josiah could just picture the gesture. He recoiled with a grimace and retreated. Better to get away while he still could.

His stomach growled again. He hurried downstairs, hoping to find Noah. Holden manned the stove, cooking bacon. He'd already finished a big pile and Josiah would dearly have liked to have a piece but knew better than to ask.

Holden liked to follow the rules, even more so with Noah gone, Josiah noticed. The older boy was as fussy as the schoolmarm, Miss Duncan, which was sort of odd. Holden had practically done cartwheels when the teacher left Sweet Willow. He'd crowed about no more school. No more books. No more rules.

None of the other boys thought that was right. Sweet Willow might not have a teacher, but the folks in charge would probably rustle up some other teacher. She might be even worse than Miss Duncan.

Josiah looked for Noah but saw no sign. His heart sank a little. Everything seemed topsy-turvy without him. Noah would be mad when he found out about the fighting but just the same, Josiah wanted him home.

A fancy lady stood beside Holden. She watched him cooking bacon with great interest. Josiah had seen her before. It took him a minute to recall where he'd seen her. Finally, he recalled seeing her at church.

She was Miss Eleanor, part of the Walker family. When he'd first seen her, he recalled thinking she looked sort of stern. Sort of highfalutin. But with her fancy dresses, she always looked like a princess, or maybe an old princess. Like an old princess who lived in an old castle. On a big hill. She probably didn't, but if she did live in a castle, he always imagined it would be one with a secret dungeon.

Miss Eleanor turned and smiled at Josiah. "And you are?"

Josiah drew back, surprised to see her smile. He knit his brow, reconsidering his prior opinion. Maybe grown-ups were right when they said you can't judge a book just because it doesn't have any good pictures, or something like that.

"Josiah, ma'am." He crossed the kitchen and held out his hand, like Noah had taught all of them. "Pleased to meet you."

"And I am very pleased to meet you."

Josiah watched Holden scoop bacon out of the sizzling pan and set it atop the stack. The older boy took the platter out of the kitchen to the dining table. Josiah scanned the kitchen for a sign of some eggs or maybe a pan of biscuits. Aside from the chocolate cake Sarah made yesterday, he saw nothing else akin to breakfast.

"Are you ready for breakfast?"

"Yes, ma'am. I'm mighty hungry."

"Good thing, because young Holden has cooked up more bacon than you can shake a stick at."

Josiah wrinkled his nose. Just bacon? Before Sarah had arrived, they'd had plenty of breakfasts that consisted solely of bacon. He hadn't minded. If anything, he'd been grateful. But his stomach had gotten used to having something to go with the bacon. He eyed the chocolate cake wistfully.

"What are you looking for?" Miss Eleanor asked.

Josiah shrugged a shoulder. "I was wondering about that chocolate cake."

Miss Eleanor smiled. She was a fancy lady, but she liked to smile. And when she smiled, it reached all the way to her eyes making them sparkle a little. Sarah smiled the same way, but Miss Eleanor's eyes sorta crinkled on the edges.

"You know," she said softly like she was talking about a secret, "I was wondering about that cake too."

"We forgot to eat it last night."

Miss Eleanor gasped, like Josiah had said they'd forgotten to feed the animals or something serious. She seemed awful surprised. He wanted to tell her that Sarah made cake all the time. But sensing a good opportunity, he knit his brow. "It might get stale."

"Now that would be a travesty, I'd say."

He wasn't quite sure if it was a travesty, but if that was something really bad, he could agree. "Sarah likes to bake fresh every afternoon. I reckon we ought to eat the cake."

"Seems prudent."

Josiah was just about to ask if that meant it was a good idea, but when she took the cake from the counter and carried it to the table, he figured that she agreed. He followed a couple of steps behind her rustling skirt. The other boys sat at the table already. Dustin glared at him, still sore about last night. He quit when he saw the cake though.

Dustin wasn't the only one surprised. Holden's jaw dropped too.

"Who wants cake with their bacon?" Miss Eleanor asked.

Of course, the boys all agreed. Even Holden mumbled something about liking cake and bacon.

Josiah glanced down the hallway, wondering if Francine was going to flounce into the dining room and ruin their breakfast. He couldn't imagine why the ladies were gathered upstairs while Sarah slept. She never slept this late. Did she get bad dreams some nights, especially with Noah gone? He wished that Noah would get home soon.

Holden made everyone quiet down so he could give thanks.

Miss Eleanor seemed to think his prayer was even nicer than eating cake and bacon for breakfast. She sat in Sarah's spot and smiled at all of them like she thought they were something special and said as much a couple of times. It made Josiah squirm when her eyes got misty. He forgot about it after a while on account of how good everything tasted. When breakfast was over, he realized he'd even forgotten to ask when Noah would get back.

Chapter Thirty-Six

Sarah

The aroma of bacon drew her from sleep. She lay in bed, wondering what time it was and why on earth someone was cooking bacon. How long had she slept?

Voices came from the bedroom corner. Was she dreaming? She sat up and instantly regretted the movement. Her head ached.

Laura sat in a chair by the window with Francine and another woman. All three looked at her with alarm. Amidst her confusion, Sarah recalled the events of the prior night. She touched her eye gingerly. It hurt less than she expected.

She would have liked to ask what Laura was doing, but first she had to be certain Dustin and the rest of the children were all right. Tossing the blankets aside, she leapt from her bed and hurried out of the room.

Stopping at the top of the stairs, she listened to yet another unfamiliar voice in the dining room.

"Snow White. That was the name I came up with. Rather clever don't you think?"

A murmur of agreement came from the boys.

What a peculiar morning. The house was full of people she didn't know. To her dismay, not one of them was Noah. He still wasn't home. She was about to call out down to ask if Dustin was there when the woman spoke again.

"It's really the perfect name, considering she's come into a home with seven menfolk. Seven! I was quite pleased when the notion came to me. Would anyone like more cake?"

The boys were eating cake. Sarah closed her eyes and tried to gather her thoughts. To her relief, she heard Dustin's voice. He asked for another slice, using his best manners, Sarah noted. She shook her head and returned to her room with the hope of trying to make sense of the bewildering morning.

Laura, Francine and the other woman stood in the middle of the room.

"Sarah," Laura said. "This is your sister, Abigail."

Her breath caught. "Oh, my."

Abigail smiled at her with tear-filled eyes. They stared at each other for a long moment. Abigail was taller than her but had similar coloring, blue eyes with blonde hair. Her hair was straight as a pin, however. Nothing like Sarah's curly, unruly mop.

Her hand drifted to her hair. Clad in a rumpled sleeping gown, a black bruise darkening her eye, her hair wild and unkept, she must have looked a sight. The moment of meeting Abigail was a far cry from what she'd imagined.

Abigail crossed the room and drew her into a tight embrace.

Sarah found herself suddenly crying. Abigail soothed her with soft words, patting her shoulder. They stood together, embracing while tears fell.

As the storm of emotions passed, Sarah laughed softly. "I'd planned to wear a blue dress when I met you."

"You look beautiful." Abigail stepped back, resting her hands upon Sarah's shoulders. "So beautiful."

A movement from the corner caught Sarah's attention. Francine gaped and shook her head with clear disagreement.

Laura whispered to the girl. Francine responded by schooling her features, trying in vain to smile agreeably.

"You always look pretty," Laura added.

"It was Holden, wasn't it?" Francine asked, pointing to her eye. "He's the worst."

"Francine, hush, child. Not now."

But Francine could hardly contain her opinions on the matter. "He's going to be in big, big trouble when Noah gets back."

Her lips curved into a smile and she snickered.

"Francine, really. Now is hardly the time." Laura put her arm around the girl's shoulders and drew her close as if that might silence her.

"It wasn't Holden," Sarah said. "He's been a tremendous help. Especially since Noah left."

Francine's smile faded. She knit her brow, clearly skeptical of Sarah's words.

"It was one of the others," Sarah said. "They were scuffling. I tried to intervene."

Laura nodded. "Francine and I should let you two girls visit. I'll send up a tray with breakfast and tend to the boys if they need anything."

The two of them left. Abigail drew her to the small sitting area by the window, keeping her arm around her shoulders as if she were a small child. Sarah relished her sister's tender touch more than she could say. The two sat on the chesterfield.

Abigail held Sarah's hands. "All my life I've dreamed of you. And now that you're here, I want to know everything."

Chapter Thirty-Seven

Noah

The light of the full moon offered enough light to make the journey home, but it was slow going. Noah brought the two palominos and the mule. He wasn't sure what he was going to do with the animals. The two horses might be ruined for all he knew. They'd been treated so harshly, there might be nothing that could be done.

The mule might have been treated harshly but most likely it was just being a mule.

It was sometime after midnight when he rode into the barnyard. He let out a weary sigh, grateful to be home. The house was dark. Everyone was asleep, most likely. He hoped so, anyway.

He hadn't slept since leaving the house and all he wanted was to get into bed, wrap his arms around his wife and sleep for a week. He wanted to check on the boys too, but after that he'd stagger off to find his sweet Sarah.

First, he tended to the horses. He untacked his horse and set aside his rifle, grateful he hadn't needed to fire the weapon. After he finished with his horse, he took the palominos to a couple of stalls at the end of the aisle, stabling them side by side in hopes that was a comfort to them.

Maybe it was a little spiteful, but he made the mule wait a spell while he fed and watered the horses. The work was slow going with no light other than the moonlight streaming through the windows.

"It's your fault the trip took so long," he muttered. "But I'll give you an extra ration of oats since you're a little thin for my liking."

The door opened. Holden appeared. He held a lantern and set it down on the stoop before coming in. "You're home. I'm real glad to see you, Noah."

"I'm mighty glad to see you, son." Noah wrapped him in a hug, tousled his hair and went back to feeding the animals.

"How did it go with the Montgomery brothers?"

"They're both dead. From an accident on a mountain path, not from gunfire. No one had to draw a gun."

Holden looked relieved, somewhat, but it was clear something was still on his mind. Thinking the boy needed more detail, he continued.

"When we found them, one brother was already dead. The other hurt himself trying to save his brother. I can't say I would have tried to save him, but the Good Lord didn't make me decide. He died a few minutes later."

Holden still had distress in his eyes, so Noah continued, hoping to say the right thing so the boy would put the memory of the Montgomery brothers behind him.

"You know, when a man's life falls apart, even the worst of men ask for God's forgiveness. Sal Montgomery, the brother we talked to, with his last breath, he asked that his brother receive a Christian burial."

"Those were bad men, Noah. They don't deserve anything like that."

"That's exactly how I feel about it too, son. But you know what? That's not for us to decide. Better to concern ourselves with our own lives, and let God decide for others, wouldn't you agree?"

"Yessir."

Holden remained standing in place, not offering to help with the mule or horses, and not saying anything more. Noah had the sense that something still troubled the boy.

"Everything all right around here?"

"Yessir. For the most part." Holden let out a deep breath, like he'd been waiting for Noah to get home so he could let it out.

"Is Sarah all right? The boys?"

"Pretty much. But I got something I need to tell you."

"What's that? Getting married? Joining the military?"

Noah grinned as he emptied a bucket of grain in the mule's bin. He might be a little delirious from the lack of sleep, but he also wanted to coax a smile from the boy. Holden always carried the weight of the world on his young shoulders.

"There was a fight, sir. Between some of the boys." He looked away, unable to keep eyes on Noah.

"That happens. S'all right."

Holden walked slowly to the nearby stall door and studied the mule.

"Watch yourself," Noah warned. "That mule bit me. Twice."

The boy hung back. "I shoulda stopped the fight. Even though you say not to get in the middle of things."

"That's how you get hurt. At least with people and dogs. Try to separate them and you'll get clobbered. Or bit. Or both."

He poured the last bucket of water for the horses. He took his rifle and ushered the boy out of the barn. Holden picked up the lantern. They walked side by side back to the house.

"Sarah tried to stop it, sir."

Noah stopped in his tracks. "Sarah..."

Holden nodded. In the dim light of the lantern, Noah watched the boy grow pale. He felt his own blood drain from his face.

"Is she hurt?"

"Sort of. She got smacked pretty good. In the eye."

"Well..." Noah tried to picture the scene but couldn't. "Is it bad?"

"She ended up with a shiner."

His stomach tightened. He couldn't imagine Sarah getting hurt, much less getting a black eye. He hurried his pace. "Who did that?"

"I'd rather not say, sir. I'll take the blame."

"Fine, don't tell me," Noah snapped. "I'll just ask Josiah."

Holden looked like he might cry. Noah regretted his tough words. They went up the steps to the house. As much as he wanted to rush inside, Noah stopped the boy at the door.

"Listen to me. You don't ever need to be afraid to tell me the truth. Ever. You boys are going to mess up. Me and Sarah will too, but we'll still be a family that loves each other. No matter what."

Holden blinked back tears. Noah knew how much it cost the boy to show any sign of weakness. A rush of emotion came over him. He felt sick about Sarah's injury. He wanted nothing more than to rush inside and make sure she was all right. But something else troubled him too, the injuries the boys bore as well, wounds he could only guess at.

"A shiner's not the end of the world," Noah said gruffly. "I've had a few myself. Some of them thanks to your Uncle Seth because that's what boys do."

Holden nodded. "Yessir."

When they went inside, Noah gestured for Holden to follow him. He went to the gun cabinet to return the rifle, leaving the cabinet open. Next, he took off his gun belt and put the revolver in the top drawer.

"My daddy gave me that gun when I turned twenty-one," he said, pointing to the rifle. "It was just a year before he died."

"It's a Trapdoor Springfield."

"That's right. Good call. One day that gun will belong to you."

Holden drew a sharp breath of surprise. His eyes widened as he looked from Noah to the gun, and back to Noah.

"You're my eldest son, after all. God might bless Sarah and me with more children. I hope so. No matter what, you'll always be my eldest son."

Holden eyes shone. He swallowed hard but didn't say a word, making Noah wonder if the notion of inheriting something like his father's gun was too much. He sensed something about the boy, that he didn't consider himself worthy of such a gift. Maybe he didn't consider himself worthy of other things either.

He closed the gun cabinet and they returned to the entry, pausing at the bottom of the stairs.

"We'll talk in the morning," Noah said quietly. "You're a good son. I thank God for you and the other boys. Every single day I thank Him."

"Thank you." The boy's words were so soft, Noah barely heard his reply.

They ascended the stairs. Noah gave Holden's shoulder a gentle pat at the top and bid him goodnight.

Taking the lantern, he went to his bedside. Sarah slept. The black eye marred her pretty face. He felt sick to his stomach to see her injury. Despite everything, he felt a surge of enormous relief.

After he washed and got ready for bed, he checked on the boys. All six, even Holden, slumbered. He returned to his room, put out the lamp and got into bed. Resisting the urge to pull Sarah into his arms, he lay in the darkness. He said a silent prayer of thanks.

Sometime in the night, Sarah came to his side and nestled in his arms as she softly murmured his name.

Chapter Thirty-Eight

Sarah

Waking before dawn, Sarah sighed with contentment. Noah had truly returned in the night. It hadn't just been a dream. As much as she wished she could linger in the shelter of his arms, she wanted to start breakfast. She wanted to serve him a hearty meal. There was no telling what he'd eaten on his journey to the Sierra Mines.

She lit the lamp and dressed hastily, stealing a few glances at Noah. Shadows played across the bed. After a few days of missing her husband, she thought he looked especially handsome. She smiled at him as he slept.

Before she left the room, she studied her reflection. The black eye was darker. Abigail and Laura both warned her it would look worse before it looked better. Touching it gently, she was surprised to find it wasn't painful. She hoped to tell Noah about the incident before the boys woke.

Downstairs, she began breakfast, starting with potatoes. The boys loved her hash browns as did Noah, but she needed to boil the potatoes before she could fry them in the skillet. Next, she kneaded dough and put two loaves into the oven.

A movement caught her attention. Noah stood in the kitchen doorway already dressed in his work clothes. He leaned against the doorframe. "I should have told you something before I left."

She drew a sharp breath of surprise and turned to face him. For a brief moment, she forgot about her darkened eye. His expression grew taut. She must look a sight.

He remained in the doorway. "I should have told you how much I love you."

"Oh, Noah." She smiled as a surge of happiness came over her.

He crossed the kitchen, closing the distance between them. "I love you, Sarah."

"And I love you," she whispered.

He brushed a lock of hair from her face.

"I wanted to tell you about this," she said.

"I heard. Holden came to the barn when I got home."

"It was my fault."

He arched a brow. "It was an accident. I understand. I still aim to talk to all the boys about what happened. Fighting's one thing, but I can't ignore someone getting hurt, especially if that someone is you."

His eyes shone with warmth. The tone he used, gentle and tender, brought a blush to her cheeks.

"Would you like to know the worst part?"

Setting his hands on her waist, he pulled her close. "I'm not sure if I do."

"I'd thought about Abigail and dreamt of meeting her for so long. I even had a dress I planned to wear. As it turns out, she arrived the morning after I got a black eye. I met her looking like this, dressed in a nightgown."

His mouth quirked. "I'm sure you looked beautiful."

"Nothing has turned out the way I planned."

He lowered to brush his lips across hers. "I reckon I could say the same. My plans didn't amount to a hill of beans, but

I've been given a mountain of joy. And for that I have to thank the good Lord."

Chapter Thirty-Nine

Noah

When he and Sarah said their vows in Galveston, the boys had grumbled about places they'd rather be, and things they'd rather be doing, and how the house was too small for someone else to live with them. Today, Noah explained there'd be no complaining when they said their vows in the church. The boys complied. Each one got dressed that morning and got along in a cheerful manner.

Caleb and Abigail came, of course, but left the three little ones with their nurse. Laura and Seth brought Francine. Noah was grateful to be surrounded by family and even more so when Beau arrived. He nodded, offering a wry grin as he sat beside Seth and Laura.

When the music began to play, Sarah appeared at the back of the church. Holden walked her down the aisle. A rush of pride came over Noah to see Holden escorting Sarah. But it was Sarah who stole his breath. She wore the white gown Laura had made. Her hair was swept into an elegant style.

The day before the wedding, Laura had sent a veil for Sarah. Abigail helped Sarah dress that morning and carefully arranged the veil to conceal Sarah's fading bruise. It was barely noticeable, but he supposed womenfolk would fret about a shiner on a wedding day. Seth joked that it might have been better if Noah had been the one with a black eye.

Pastor James conducted the ceremony. The young pastor had teased both Sarah and Noah about the notion of a second wedding. He'd had a glint of amusement in his eye that morning, but now stood before them solemn and reverent.

Noah held her hands and gazed into her eyes, obscured somewhat by the veil. Her hands trembled. Her eyes shone with tender emotion that warmed his heart.

When the pastor gave his permission, Noah lifted the veil slowly and let it fall. He cupped her chin and kissed her sweet smiling lips. He lingered longer than the first time he'd kissed her, but not as long as he would have liked.

Later, outside the church, Pastor James congratulated them but couldn't resist teasing a little more. "This is the first time I married a couple for the second time."

Sarah blushed a pretty pink, bringing a smile to Noah's lips.

"I'd always imagined a church wedding," she said shyly. "I suppose it's something young girls dream of. Not just the dress, of course, but saying their vows before God."

Pastor James chuckled. "It was an honor to do my part. I'm so pleased to see Noah found not just a wife but a mother to the boys."

"It means the world to me to have my sister with me on such a special day," Sarah added, casting a glance toward Abigail.

Noah kept Sarah's hand in his but let his gaze drift to where the boys sat on a bench. All six. They talked amongst themselves without any jostling or arguing. When Josiah spoke, he gestured broadly, probably exaggerating wildly, but the other five listened respectfully. None of the other five told him to hush or taunted the boy.

Noah felt a surge of pride to see them behaving like young gentlemen. They'd always been good-hearted boys, but somewhere along the way, they'd become civilized. Why, Dustin had even managed to drag a comb through his hair.

Sarah's gentle grace wrought a change over the boys, over him, over everything.

The families, riding in a caravan of buggies, horses, and buckboards, made their way to Seth and Laura's ranch to enjoy the wedding meal Laura and Francine had prepared. The boys piled in the back, joking and laughing.

The sun shone, chasing the morning chill. A light breeze blew. It swept across the fields, turning the lush grass into an ocean of rippling, green waves.

"Fine day for a wedding," Noah said over the rumble of wheels.

Sarah nodded. "It's lovely. Texas grows prettier to me every day."

Beau came to the side of the buckboard, riding one of the geldings Noah had given him. "Never thought I'd see the day. Noah Bailey standing at the front of a church, saying his vows."

"Sending for Sarah was the best thing I ever did." Noah gestured to the back of the buckboard. "Right along with taking in a passel of rascals."

"Is there a lady in your life?" Sarah asked.

"No, ma'am."

Noah heard the firm edge in Beau's response. He noted the way Sarah's lips tilted up. She'd heard it too and regarded Beau's tone as a challenge. She straightened her shoulders and kept her gaze fixed forward with a bemused smile.

When they arrived at the house, Sarah sent the boys to wash. After everyone had settled to eat lunch, Seth said a blessing over the food. He thanked God for the meal, for Sarah and Noah and for the boys.

Eleanor, sitting next to Sarah, murmured, "we're so glad you're here, Snow White."

Chapter Forty

Sarah

As the long days of summer drifted toward fall, Noah and Sarah prepared for the boys' new year at school. Each boy needed a haircut, shoes and trousers. Their Aunt Laura promised new shirts for them.

The morning of the first school day dawned bright and with a hint of chill in the September air. The boys did their chores early. Sarah fed them a hearty breakfast. While they ate, she prepared their lunch buckets. Each boy got two sandwiches, an apple, and three oatmeal cookies.

She cooked a ham the evening before. That morning she baked extra bread along with the cookies. The boys smiled appreciatively at the aromas wafting through the house.

Their voices held a note of excitement.

Holden, who'd started the summer grumbling about school, seemed pleased to be returning. His reading had improved tremendously, a fact which made both Sarah and Holden proud. They no longer read together in the evenings, but the boy continued to read on his own, borrowing a new book from Sarah every few days.

Noah wandered into the kitchen and wrapped his arms around her as she packed the last of the lunches.

"Just between you and me, I sorta miss them when they go to school."

"I'll miss them too," Sarah confessed.

Noah set his hand on her stomach. She smiled and covered his hand with hers. They stood in silence by the window. Leaning back, she sank into the shelter of his embrace. He spread his fingers across her waist. Their nest was growing with a new child arriving in the spring, God-willing.

He turned her to face him. Lowering to brush a kiss across her lips, he tightened his hold and gently caressed her shoulder. His kiss was gentle, lingering and as tender as his words.

"Sure like the feel of you in my arms," Noah whispered. "Especially at night. I sleep better when you rest your head on my shoulder."

"I sleep better too. I never imagined how much comfort I'd find sleeping next to you."

His eyes filled with soft warmth. "Me neither. When I set out to get married, I thought it was to fix something for the boys. They seemed like little puzzles, each one with a piece missing."

She held her breath, wondering where he might take the conversation. He'd never said anything like this before. He went on in the same solemn, heartfelt tone.

"I never imagined," he whispered, "that I was the one missing a piece. Maybe a few pieces. When I prayed for a wife, the good Lord knew just what I needed."

Sarah blinked back the tears that threatened to spill from her eyes. "He knew what I needed too. I came looking for a sister and He gave me so much more. He gave me a family."

"I'm very grateful," he said.

"I am as well."

The boys' voices drifted through the open window. She half-expected Noah to end the kiss, but he held her close as if not ready to part. Usually, he saved his kisses for the privacy of their bedroom. They rarely risked a kiss while standing before a window.

Whenever the boys saw a display of affection, they'd become mortified. Their dismay amused Noah and Sarah, but they both agreed not to kiss or embrace in front of the boys to spare them any further embarrassment.

"Where's Noah?" Josiah called from somewhere outside.

Noah chuckled and smiled down at her. A rush of warmth heated her face.

Noah's eyes twinkled as if he could read her thoughts. He kissed her on the forehead. "Not feeling poorly this morning?" he asked.

"I believe I'm all done with morning sickness."

"If it troubles you again, I want you to stay in bed. Clear?"

She smiled at the protective note in his voice. "Who will make breakfast and pack lunches if I'm sleeping the morning away?"

"I suppose the boys would have to manage with whatever I rustle up."

She turned back to finish her task of packing lunches but heard the note of humor in his voice. He leaned down to brush a kiss across her cheek while snatching a cookie from the nearby basket.

"You rascal," she murmured, shaking her head.

He moved to the window and searched for a sign of the boys who were harnessing the team. "I figure you'll have a little extra time today to make more cookies."

Sarah tucked a linen napkin across the top of each bucket. "I must keep busy. I owe letters to several friends, and I have two unopened letters from Gertie and Bess. After we take the boys, I plan on writing at least one letter."

Noah offered a mischievous grin as he grabbed another cookie.

Before she could fuss about the cookie thievery, the boys came up the path with the horses and wagon. Sarah put on her bonnet and Noah helped her carry the buckets out.

Holden and Dustin both rode alongside the wagon, mounted on the two palominos. When Noah brought the horses, he'd told the boys the animals might not be fit for riding. The Montgomery brothers had abused them.

The boys had taken his comments as a challenge. They'd worked tirelessly trying to earn the trust of the frightened animals. Over days and weeks, they'd transformed the poor creatures. Sarah's heart filled with pride to see the boys astride the gentled horses.

Noah helped Sarah aboard the wagon. Soon they were on their way.

Holden rode beside them. "This is my last year," he told Sarah, a note of pride in his voice. "Next year, I'll be helping Noah."

"That's right," Noah said. "Just make sure you don't give the teacher a bad time. None of your pranks. We don't want the Bailey boys to run off another teacher."

"You mean *teachers*," Dustin said, coming along the other side of the wagon.

"There are two of them?" Holden asked. "I hadn't heard about two teachers."

"They probably had to hire another one on account of our family," Noah grumbled.

Holden gave a sheepish grin but didn't object to Noah's comment. His grin faded as he knit his brow. "Did you hear about this from Francine?"

"Nope. Doyle told Walt at the auction yesterday. Walt told me," Dustin said pleased to be the bearer of news.

Holden looked slightly less convinced.

Sarah spoke. "It shouldn't matter one way or the other, boys. I hope you make the new teacher or teachers feel welcome. I intend to pay a social call to the school regularly."

Both boys and Noah looked surprised. Sarah chuckled, amused by their dismay. She adjusted her bonnet. She hoped the promise of visiting the school would give the boys pause. They drove the rest of the way in quiet, the boys casting furtive glances her direction.

By the time they arrived at the small schoolhouse, it was a hive of activity. Families had come from Sweet Willow and the surrounding countryside to bring their children to school. There was a festive air amongst the parents and children alike.

People gathered to discuss farming, the railroad, and the price of various crops. They milled about, waiting for school to start, visiting with folks they might not have seen in some time.

Noah hitched the wagon as the children clambered down from the buckboard. Before they ran off to find their friends, he made them gather round. They stood under a grove of oak trees with hands joined as Noah said a prayer with the children. He thanked God for the school and the teachers and asked for His guidance and blessings for the coming year.

Sarah's eyes prickled as she listened to his voice. She added her own silent prayer of thanksgiving, thanking the Lord for her husband and boys. Noah finished the prayer.

"Amen," he said, his voice deep and unwavering. The boys chorused his amen with their own. Setting their caps on their head, they hurried off to join the other children. Noah kept her hand in his as they strolled amongst their friends and neighbors.

Seth and Laura arrived on the buckboard and waved a friendly greeting. Francine rode between them, dressed in a pretty frock the color of a robin's egg. She wore a broad smile and waved to Holden.

Noah and Sarah shared a look of surprise.

"I'll be," Noah muttered.

The schoolhouse doors were closed for now. Inside, there was some movement, however, signs of the teachers preparing for the first day. The doors opened at last. Two ladies appeared, one carrying a handbell, which she started ringing. The children chattered excitedly.

Sarah stared in surprise. The two teachers looked familiar, very familiar. After a moment's confusion, Sarah realized who they were. One of them waved and nudged her companion, who cupped her hand to her mouth and called a greeting.

"Gertie and Bess," Sarah murmured. "I can hardly believe my eyes."

"Come again?" said Noah.

She took his hand and led him to the front of the schoolhouse. "Gertie and Bess are my friends from the ship. The two ladies who helped me."

Sarah would have liked to visit with the two ladies, but it was impossible to even say a proper hello. There was too much commotion. Everyone in Sweet Willow wanted to greet the new teachers, it seemed. Sarah gave each a quick hug and a promise to catch up in the coming days. Both ladies gave Noah a smile and nod before returning to their charges.

The day was busy. Her plans to write letters had to be postponed. It wasn't until later that evening, in the quiet of her room, that Sarah had a chance to read their letter. Much of it she could already guess. Just the same, it pleased her to read about the women's plans to come to Sweet Willow.

Dusk fell, casting shadows across her desk. She lit a lamp as she considered answering a letter to friends in California. Music from a guitar drifted through the open window. It came from the porch downstairs. She crossed the room and listened to Noah and Holden talking quietly. Noah instructed Holden on a new chord. She couldn't make out their conversation, just the general gist of their exchange.

Holden strummed his gentle melody. She hadn't heard him play this tune, but the music was lovely. Heartfelt. It filled her chest with warmth. Ever since she'd found that she was expecting, certain moments during her day struck her with a poignancy she'd never known. The tender song made her eyes sting with the threat of tears.

She chided herself, grateful that Noah wasn't there to see her sway of emotions. She wiped her eyes. Tugging the window up another few inches, she took in the sweet song. Holden would play a spell and then stop to ask Noah a question. Noah answered, his voice a deep baritone, with words Sarah couldn't make out.

Sarah liked to let Noah talk with the boys without her sometimes. Not once had any of them told her she wasn't welcome, but she felt it important to let them be. Perhaps it was just a notion she had fixed in her mind, a sense of holding back so the boys could have Noah to themselves.

The boys loved her. She knew that. But a mother's love differed from that of a father.

Without thinking, she brushed her fingers across her stomach.

Noah had told the boys about the baby just last week. Sarah had fretted beforehand. How would they greet the prospect of a new child? To her surprise and delight, all six boys were very pleased. They'd been confused about how long it took for a mother to bring a child into the world. When Sarah explained the baby would arrive in the spring, it had disappointed them. The spring was so far off. Why, they'd be in a whole new year by then.

The conversation quickly turned to more interesting things, such as the fine spotted bass Walt almost caught a few days prior. A debate ensued as to the size of the fish and how close Walt had come to landing the giant creature.

She'd expected a hundred questions, but as it turned out, a baby didn't interest them as much as a story of a fish. Especially if the baby's arrival was eons away. She'd sat in bewildered silence while the boys argued and scoffed and disputed Walt's claims about the errant bass.

Down on the porch, Holden stopped his music. Noah said good night to the boys. The last rays of twilight dimmed. Sarah closed the window and drew the curtains.

Instead of writing a letter, Sarah prepared for bed. She donned a wrapper, went to the kitchen to be certain she had enough eggs for breakfast. After finishing her task, she returned upstairs and said goodnight to the boys. Josiah was already fast asleep. Dustin dozed, and the rest of them were moments away from drifting off.

Only Holden was still up. She found him in the hallway, dressed in his pajamas, packing his school satchel.

"Off to bed?" she asked.

"Yes, ma'am. We can't get to school late." His eyes widened. "The new teachers sort of scare all of us."

Sarah stifled a smile. "I don't doubt it. Gertie and Bessie Payne are a force to be reckoned with."

Holden nodded. "None of us want to step one inch out of line. Not one inch."

"Seems prudent."

"Francine thinks they're the best teachers in the world." He narrowed his eyes. "They love her. Little teacher's pet."

Sarah shook her head. "I'm sure neither of them will play favorites."

Holden grumbled. She kissed him on the forehead. He bid her goodnight and went to his room, yawning twice before reaching the door.

"Say your prayers," she called softly.

"Yes, ma'am."

Returning to her room, Sarah found Noah as he prepared for bed.

Noah buttoned his pajama shirt. "Did you know Holden's writing songs?"

"I heard you down there." Sarah sat at her dressing table and brushed her hair. "I didn't realize he was working on his own songs."

Noah crossed the room, coming to a stop behind her. "He's writing a lullaby."

"A lullaby!" Sarah was so surprised that she dropped her hairbrush. She turned to pick it up, but Noah set a hand on her shoulder to stop her.

Instead of giving it back to her, he began brushing her hair. "A lullaby for the baby."

"That's so sweet," she marveled.

"He confessed that he had worried about us having kids in the beginning. He fretted that we wouldn't want them if we started having our own children."

For the second time that evening, Sarah's eyes prickled.

When she learned that she was expecting, the news had filled her with joy. She understood the boys might not view the news with the same happiness. It pained her. She didn't know what to say, or if she should just let it be.

Noah sighed. "I explained that you and I aren't *starting* to have our own children. We already have six. We're just having another. That's all."

His voice was soft. His eyes held a gentle light. Sarah blinked, trying in vain to keep the tears from falling, to no avail.

Noah went on. "Then I told him about God's love for us."

Her breath left her throat with a soft sigh. It was difficult to reply. She felt overcome. Her throat tightened. She took a handkerchief from the table and dabbed her eyes.

Noah went on, unconcerned about her tears. "I told him that God's love isn't like a peach pie."

Sarah paused. Her jaw dropped a notch as she tried to fathom where this might lead.

"And God's love is perfect, but maybe a parent's love isn't like a peach pie either."

"A peach pie?" Her thoughts spun as she tried to recall the times she'd made peach pie. There'd been no conversation about God, or love, or children as far as she could remember.

"You know when you make a pie, we have to divide it up because there's only a certain amount. Love isn't that way. It doesn't have limits." He set the brush aside and rested his hands on the chair. "Love bears all things, believes all things, hopes all things, endures all things. Love never fails."

"Corinthians," she whispered.

With a nod, he lowered the lamp's wick and led her to the bed. She settled in her usual spot next to him and rested her head on his shoulder. He wrapped his arm around her and pulled her closer. To rest in his arms at the end of the day always filled her heart with peace. Her tears dried. She let out a contented sigh when he kissed the top of her head.

He spoke softly. "And now abide faith, hope, love, these three; but the greatest of these is love."

Chapter Forty-One

Beau Bailey

Beau made his way down the train car, pausing at each compartment to eye the passengers. Miners and young cowboys filled the second-class car. The first-class car held a more refined crowd, mostly older gentlemen traveling with their wives.

He didn't see any sign of the thieves. Good thing too. The Craddick brothers didn't bother with guns when they robbed a train. In tight spaces, they always preferred knives.

When he checked the compartments, he often noted the same alarmed response. He was used to frightening folks. Men glared. Women cried out in fright. He'd tap his badge to show he was a trusted lawman, a Texas Ranger. Usually, the badge would ease their fears.

Either way, the fine folks in first class always seemed relieved when he nodded and moved on. As he approached the end of the car, he found a few empty compartments. He checked under the seats but found no sign of the outlaws.

One more compartment and he could consider his work done for the evening. The Texas Eagle wouldn't stop till morning. It was growing clear that the Craddick brothers weren't on this train. He moved cautiously to inspect the last compartment. When he looked inside, he found only one passenger. A woman. A young woman.

He stood in the doorway and studied her with curiosity. She sat by the window, reading a novel. With the sun sinking in the west, soft rays of sunshine lit the interior. The woman was so absorbed in her book she didn't notice him standing three steps away.

Her lack of awareness gave him the chance to admire her beauty. Coppery locks swept into an elegant arrangement, one that showed off her pale, creamy skin. Her narrow shoulders accentuated her feminine form. She knit her brow as she read, forming two small lines between arched brows. Her book caused some concern, judging from the way she bit the edge of her lower lip.

Transfixed, he remained in the doorway, watching with a mix of interest and bemusement.

Her perfect posture made him sure she'd gone to some fancy finishing school. Her dress looked freshly pressed unlike the other ladies on the train. They all wore rumpled dresses and looked shabby in comparison.

She continued reading. The train rumbled. She was completely unaware of a stranger watching her. Good thing he wasn't an outlaw. He could have robbed her three times over by now, and with all the racket, not one other passenger would have been the wiser.

A wash of irritation heated his thoughts. The girl was vulnerable, traveling alone through remote and desolate Texas lands. How had any self-respecting father, brother or husband allowed such a lovely and delicate woman to set out on her own?

He removed his hat and shifted his gun belt back a notch so it wouldn't cause alarm. Next, he raked his fingers through his hair. Why he did that, he couldn't say.

"Miss," he said quietly, hoping not to startle her.

She looked up, blinked a few times and smiled politely. "I've already shown my ticket."

He tapped his badge. "I'm a Ranger."

She studied his badge before lifting her gaze to meet his. "What's a Ranger?"

Frowning, he stepped inside the compartment. "I work for the state of Texas. I'm a lawman."

Her eyes lit with surprise. "Oh my."

"Where are you traveling to?"

"I'm traveling to Sweet William." She closed her book and set it down. Taking a deep breath, it seemed she was summoning her nerve to say more. "I'm a mail-order bride."

Her cheeks colored a delicate pink. He watched as the blush bloomed across her fair skin. Rubbing the back of his neck, he grimaced and wondered what in tarnation was wrong with him. It wasn't like him to dwell on the way a girl blushed.

"Do you mean Sweet Willow?"

Her color deepened. "Yes, I believe you're right. Do you know the town?"

"I do, in fact. I have family there." He gestured to the seat across from her. "May I?"

"Of course," she said shyly.

They rode in silence for a spell. Some females might be skittish about a lawman inviting himself to sit with them. She seemed a tad nervous, but not overly fretful. Every so often she stole a glance.

"It might be best if you have company," he said. "I aim to make certain your trip is comfortable and, above all, safe."

Her eyes widened. Her throat tightened as she swallowed. There it was. The fear. He saw it in people's eyes more often than he liked, especially when he talked with folks one on one. People had good reason to be wary of him and his fellow

Rangers. There were plenty of Rangers who took advantage of the weak. Some who were as black hearted as the outlaws they hunted. Not Beau. He'd dedicated his life to protecting the innocent and had the scars to prove it.

"You can rest assured I mean no harm," he said.

She nodded slowly as if not entirely sure if she should trust him.

The girl wore a floral fragrance. Just a hint. Not heavy like many other ladies. Annoyance jabbed at him. He wondered about the lucky man waiting for her. He wanted to ask the man's name but refrained. Heck, he didn't even know *her* name.

"My name's Beau Bailey."

"Pleased to meet you. My name is Susanna Astor."

"Astor," he remarked with surprise.

She shook her head. "I need to remember I'm married now. My last name is Anderson."

Anderson? That was an even greater surprise than Astor. A murmur of surprise fell from his mouth. Thankfully the noisy train drowned out the sound. He knew of two men in Sweet Willow by the name of Anderson. Brothers. Will and Robert. Two cantankerous and very elderly bachelors who despised each other and just about everyone else with a deep and abiding hatred.

Despite their mutual loathing, the brothers lived side by side in two ramshackle shacks. They had more money than Solomon, but you wouldn't know it from the looks of things around the Anderson Ranch.

The men were bad-tempered. And old enough to be Susanna's grandfather. He wondered if she realized how old her husband was. Why would either of them take a wife?

He stared in disbelief. It was impossible to comprehend. How could this sweet young woman have married one of those men? His mind rebelled, refusing to accept the idea. The marriage probably came about because of the men's unending quarrels. One of the brothers probably took a wife just to spite the other.

"I'll be," he muttered. He wanted to whisk her away from Will and Robert Anderson. He indulged in the notion of sheltering her from harm.

Noting his dismay, Susanna averted her eyes and turned away to look out the window. The last rays of dusk cast a soft glow over her features. He could hardly tear his eyes from her. He forced himself to look away.

He recalled visiting his cousin Noah. He'd stayed for dinner, sharing a meal with Noah, his new wife and adopted boys. During the meal, Holden, Noah's eldest son, told of an event at the family's auction barn.

The story concerned the two Anderson brothers. They'd become embroiled in a bidding war over an Angus bull. Their tempers flared as usual. The argument was absurd. They lived on the same ranch. Their animals were all part of the same herd. That logic didn't slow the men down, however.

A crowd gathered to see who would get the winning bid.

As the story reached its climax, Josiah, Noah's youngest, interrupted Holden. He stood up, knocking over his chair and finished the tale. "And then, wouldn't you know, Will Anderson keels over, dead. *Dead*. Dead I tell you. Dead as a doorknob!"

The boys snickered, covering their mouths with their hands. They didn't want to laugh at a story about a man meeting his maker. The poor man had died while trying to win a bid on a bull he probably didn't even want.

267

Just the same, Josiah's comment about doorknobs amused them.

Even better, the phrase sparked a fine debate. Was it dead as a doorknob, or dead as a doornail? No one could say, exactly. One of them suggested dead as a dodo. Even Noah had joined the lively discussion while his wife merely sighed and shook her head.

Beau thought about the evening. He was almost certain the boys had said it was Will Anderson that had died. Or was it Robert? Beau pushed the memory aside. He'd be certain to find out more when the train arrived in Sweet Willow.

Setting his hat aside, he leaned forward to rest his elbows on his knees. "Have you met Mr. Anderson?"

"No. I haven't. We married by proxy."

"Is that so? I've never met anyone who married by proxy. Seems sort of risky. Especially for the lady." He wasn't sure why he was questioning her actions. It was none of his business. None at all.

She drew herself up. "I've been swindled before, Mr. Bailey. Cheated by my own flesh and blood, which is precisely why I wished to leave Albany. I told Mr. Anderson I wouldn't come to Texas without marrying."

A frightened look came over her. It vanished as quickly as it had appeared. She pursed her lips and lifted her chin as if reminding herself she was an Astor. Or had once been an Astor. "I'm sorry, Mr. Bailey. I don't know what's come over me. I shouldn't trouble you with silly stories."

He schooled his features into a casual smile. "It's not silly at all. I wish you all the best."

His words weren't exactly heartfelt. Not in the least. He intended to learn more of her circumstances. He told himself it was a work matter. He was a Texas Ranger, after all. A man dedicated to justice and protecting the innocent. The fragile look in her lovely, pale grey eyes had nothing to do with his motives. Nothing at all.

The End